THE DEATH OF JESUS

ALSO BY J. M. COETZEE

Dusklands

In the Heart of the Country

Waiting for the Barbarians

Life & Times of Michael K

Foe

White Writing

Age of Iron

Doubling the Point: Essays and Interviews

The Master of Petersburg

Giving Offense

Boyhood

The Lives of Animals

Disgrace

Stranger Shores: Essays 1986–1999

Youth

Elizabeth Costello

Slow Man

Inner Workings

Diary of a Bad Year

Summertime

Scenes from Provincial Life

The Childhood of Jesus

(with Paul Auster) *Here and Now: Letters, 2008–2011*

(with Arabella Kurtz) *The Good Story:*
Exchanges on Truth, Fiction and Psychotherapy

J. M. COETZEE

The Death of Jesus

Harvill *Secker*

LONDON

1 3 5 7 9 10 8 6 4 2

Harvill Secker, an imprint of Vintage,
20 Vauxhall Bridge Road,
London SW1V 2SA

Harvill Secker is part of the Penguin Random House group of companies
whose addresses can be found at global.penguinrandomhouse.com.

Copyright © J. M. Coetzee 2019

First published by Harvill Secker in 2020
First published by Text Publishing in Australia in 2019

Penguin.co.uk/vintage

A CIP catalogue record for this book is available from the British Library

ISBN 9781787302112

Printed and bound in Great Britain by Clays Ltd, Elcograf S.p.A.

Penguin Random House is committed to a sustainable future
for our business, our readers and our planet. This book is made
from Forest Stewardship Council® certified paper.

THE DEATH OF JESUS

CHAPTER 1

IT IS a crisp autumn afternoon. On the grassy expanse behind the apartment block he stands watching a game of football. Usually he is the sole spectator of these games played between children from the block. But today two strangers have stopped to watch too: a man in a dark suit with, by his side, a girl in school uniform.

The ball loops out to the left wing, where David is playing. Trapping the ball, David easily outsprints the defender who comes out to engage him and lofts the ball into the centre. It escapes everyone, escapes the goalkeeper, crosses the goal line.

In these weekday games there are no proper teams. The boys divide up as they see fit, drop in, drop out. Sometimes there are thirty on the field, sometimes only half a dozen. When David first joined in, three years ago, he was the youngest and smallest. Now he is among the bigger boys, but nimble despite his height, quick on his feet, a deceptive runner.

There is a lull in the game. The two strangers approach; the dog slumbering at his feet rouses himself and raises his head.

'Good day,' says the man. 'What teams are these?'

'It is just a pick-up game between children from the neighbourhood.'

'They are not bad,' says the stranger. 'Are you a parent?'

Is he a parent? Is it worth trying to explain what exactly he is? 'That is my son over there,' he says. 'David. The tall boy with the dark hair.'

The stranger inspects David, the tall boy with the dark hair, who is strolling about abstractedly, not paying much attention to the game.

'Have they thought of organizing themselves into a team?' says the stranger. 'Let me introduce myself. My name is Julio Fabricante. This is Maria Prudencia. We are from Las Manos. Do you know Las Manos? No? It is the orphanage on the far side of the river.'

'Simón,' says he, Simón. He shakes hands with Julio Fabricante from the orphanage, gives Maria Prudencia a nod. Maria is, he would guess, fourteen years old, solidly built, with heavy eyebrows and a well-developed bust.

'I ask because we would be happy to host them. We have a proper field with proper markings and proper goalposts.'

'I think they are content just kicking a ball around.'

'You do not improve without competition,' says Julio.

'Agreed. On the other hand, forming a team would mean selecting eleven and excluding the rest, which would contradict the ethos they have built up. That is how I see it. But maybe I am wrong. Maybe they would indeed like to compete and improve. Ask them.'

David has the ball at his feet. He feints left and goes right, making the move so fluidly that the defender is stranded. He passes the ball to a teammate and watches as the teammate lobs it tamely into the goalkeeper's arms.

'He is very good, your son,' says Julio. 'A natural.'

'He has an advantage over his friends. He takes dancing lessons, so he has good balance. If the other boys took dancing lessons they would be just as good.'

'You hear that, Maria?' says Julio. 'Maybe you should follow David's lead and take dancing lessons.'

Maria stares fixedly ahead.

'Maria Prudencia plays football,' says Julio. 'She is one of the stalwarts of our team.'

The sun is going down. Soon the boy who owns the ball will reclaim it ('I've got to go') and the players will drift off home.

'I know you are not their coach,' says Julio. 'I can also see you are not in favour of organized sport. Nevertheless, for the boys' sake, give it some thought. Here is my card. They might enjoy it, playing as a team against another team. Very good to meet you.'

Dr Julio Fabricante, Educador, says the card. *Orfanato de Las Manos, Estrella 4*.

'Come, Bolívar,' he says. 'Time to go home.'

The dog heaves himself to his feet, letting loose a malodorous fart.

Over supper David asks: 'Who was the man you were talking to?'

'His name is Dr Julio Fabricante. Here is his card. He is from an orphanage. He proposes that you boys choose a team to play against a team from the orphanage.'

Inés examines the card. '*Educador*,' she says. 'What is that?'

'It is a fancy word for teacher.'

When he arrives at the grassy field the following afternoon, Dr Fabricante is already there, addressing the boys clustered around him. 'You can also choose a name for your team,' he is saying. 'And you can choose the colour of your team shirts.'

'Los Gatos,' says one boy.

'Las Panteras,' says another.

Las Panteras finds favour among the boys, who seem excited by Dr Julio's proposal.

'We at the orphanage call ourselves Los Halcones, after the hawk, the bird with the keenest sight of all.'

David speaks: 'Why don't you call yourselves Los Huérfanos?'

There is an awkward silence. 'Because, young man,' says Dr Fabricante, 'we do not seek any favours. We do not ask to be allowed to win just because of who we are.'

'Are you an orphan?' asks David.

'No, I do not happen to be an orphan myself, but I am in charge of the orphanage and live there. I have great respect and love for orphans, of whom there are many more in the world than you may think.'

The boys fall silent. He, Simón, keeps his silence too.

'I am an orphan,' says David. 'Can I play for your team?'

The boys titter. They are used to David's provocations. 'Stop it, David!' hisses one of them.

It is time for him to intervene. 'I am not sure, David, that you appreciate what it is to be an orphan, a real orphan. An orphan has no family, no home. That is where Dr Julio comes in. He offers orphans a home. You already have a home.' He turns to Dr Julio.

'I apologize for involving you in a family dispute.'

'No need to apologize. The question young David raises is an important one. What does it mean to be an orphan? Does it simply mean that you are without visible parents? No. To be an orphan, at the deepest level, is to be alone in the world. So in a sense we are all orphans, for we are all, at the deepest level, alone in the world. As I say to the young people in my charge, there is nothing to be ashamed of in living in an orphanage, for an orphanage is a microcosm of society.'

'You didn't answer me,' says David. 'Can I play for your team?'

'It would be better if you played for your own team,' says Dr Fabricante. 'If everyone played for Los Halcones there would be no one for us to play against. There would be no competition.'

'I am not asking for everyone. I am just asking for me.'

Dr Fabricante turns to him, Simón. 'What do you think, señor? Do you approve of Las Panteras as a name for your football team?'

'I have no opinion,' he replies. 'I would not wish to impose my tastes on these young folk.' He stops there. He would like to add: *These young folk who were happy playing football in their own way until you arrived on the scene.*

CHAPTER 2

THIS IS the fourth year of their residence in the apartment block. Though Inés's apartment on the second floor is large enough for all three of them, he has by mutual agreement taken an apartment of his own on the ground floor, smaller and more simply furnished. He has been able to afford it ever since his earnings were augmented with a disability grant for a back injury that has never properly healed, an injury dating from his time as a stevedore in Novilla.

He has an income of his own and an apartment of his own but he has no social circle, not because he is an unsociable being or because Estrella is an unfriendly town but because he resolved long ago to devote himself without reserve to the boy's upbringing. As for Inés, she spends her days and sometimes her evenings too attending to the fashion boutique she half owns. Her friends are drawn from Modas Modernas and the wider world of fashion. He is deliberately incurious about these friendships. Whether among her friends she has lovers he does not know and does not care to know, so long as she remains a good mother.

Under their wing David has flourished. He is strong and

healthy. Years ago, when they were living in Novilla, they had a battle with the public school system. David's teachers found him *obstinado*, intractable. Since then they have kept him out of the public schools.

He, Simón, is confident that a child with such clear inborn intelligence can do without formal schooling. *He is an exceptional child*, he tells Inés. *Who can predict in what direction his gifts will lie?* Inés, in her more generous moments, is prepared to agree.

At the Academy of Music in Estrella David attends classes in singing and dancing. The singing classes are supervised by the director of the Academy, Juan Sebastián Arroyo. When it comes to dancing, there is no one at the Academy who has anything to teach him. On the days when he makes an appearance in class, he dances as he chooses; the rest of the students follow or, if they cannot follow, watch.

He, Simón, is a dancer too, though a late convert and without any gifts. He does his dancing in private, in the evenings, alone. After donning his pyjamas, he plays the gramophone at a subdued level and dances for himself, with his eyes shut, long enough for his mind to go blank. Then he switches off the music and goes to bed and sleeps the sleep of the just.

The music is, most evenings, a suite of dances for flute and violin composed by Arroyo to mark the death of his second wife, Ana Magdalena. The dances have no title; the record, pressed in the back room of a shop in the city, has no label. The music itself is slow and stately and sad.

David does not deign to attend normal classes, and in particular to do arithmetical exercises like a normal ten-year-old, because of a prejudice against arithmetic encouraged in him by the deceased señora Arroyo, who impressed it on students who passed through her hands that integral numbers are divinities, heavenly entities who existed before the physical world came into being and will continue to exist after the world has come to an end, and therefore deserve reverence. To mix the numbers one with another (*adición, sustracción*), or chop them into pieces (*fracciones*), or apply them to measuring quantities of bricks or flour (*la medida*), constitutes an affront to their divinity.

For his tenth birthday he and Inés gave David a watch, which David refuses to wear because (he says) it fixes the numbers in a circular order. Nine o'clock may be before ten o'clock, he says, but nine is neither before nor after ten.

To señora Arroyo's devotion to the numbers, given form in the dances she taught her students, David has added an idiosyncratic twist of his own: identification of particular numbers with particular stars in the sky.

He, Simón, does not understand the philosophy of number (which he privately considers to be not a philosophy but a cult) proselytized at the Academy: openly by the late señora, more discreetly by the widower Arroyo and his musician friends. He does not understand it but he tolerates it, not only out of consideration for David but also because, when he is in the right mood, during his solitary dancing of an evening, there sometimes comes to him a vision, momentary, transient, of what señora Arroyo used to speak of: silvery spheres too many to count rotating about each other with an unearthly hum, in unending space.

He dances, he has visions, yet he does not think of himself as a convert to the cult of number. For his visions he has a reasoned explanation, one that satisfies him most of the time: the lulling rhythm of the dance, the hypnotic chant of the flute, induce a state of trance in which fragments are sucked up from the bed of memory and whirled before the inner eye.

David cannot or will not do sums. More worryingly, he will not read. That is to say, having taught himself to read out of *Don Quixote*, he shows no interest in reading any other book. He knows *Don Quixote* by heart, in an abbreviated version for children; he treats it not as a made-up story but as a veritable history. Somewhere in the world, or if not in this world then in the next one, Don Quixote is abroad, mounted on his steed Rocinante, with Sancho trotting by his side on an ass.

They have had arguments about *Don Quixote*, he and the boy. If you would only open yourself to other books, he says, you will find that the world has a multitude of heroes besides the Don, and heroines too, conjured out of nothing by the fertile minds of authors. Indeed, being a gifted child, you could make up heroes of your own and send them out into the world to have adventures.

David barely listens to him. 'I don't want to read other books,' he says dismissively. 'I can already read.'

'You have a false understanding of what it means to read. Reading is not just turning printed signs into sounds. Reading is something deeper. True reading means hearing what the book has to say and pondering it – perhaps even having a conversation in your mind with the author. It means learning about the world – the world as it really is, not as you wish it to be.'

'Why?' says David.

'Why? Because you are young and ignorant. You will rid yourself of your ignorance only by opening yourself to the world. And the best way of opening yourself to the world is to read what other people have to say, people less ignorant than you.'

'I know about the world.'

'No, you do not. You know nothing whatsoever of the world outside your own limited field of experience. Dancing and kicking a football are fine activities in themselves but they do not teach you about the world.'

'I read *Don Quixote*.'

'*Don Quixote*, I repeat, is not the world. Far from it. *Don Quixote* is a made-up story of a deluded old man. It is an amusing book, it sucks you into its fantasy, but fantasy is not real. Indeed, the message of the book is precisely to warn readers like yourself against being sucked into an unreal world, a world of fantasy, as Don Quixote is sucked. Do you not recall how the book ends, with Don Quixote coming to his senses and telling his niece to burn his books so that no one in future will be tempted to follow his crazy path?'

'But she doesn't burn his books.'

'She does! It may not say so in the book, but she does! She is only too thankful to get rid of them.'

'But she doesn't burn *Don Quixote*.'

'She can't burn *Don Quixote* because she is inside *Don Quixote*. You can't burn a book if you are inside it, if you are a character in it.'

'You can. But she doesn't. Because if she did I would not have *Don Quixote*. It would be burnt up.'

He comes away from these disputations with the boy baffled yet obscurely proud: baffled because he cannot overcome a ten-year-old in an argument; proud because the ten-year-old can so deftly tie him in knots. *The child may be lazy, the child may be arrogant*, he tells himself, *but at least the child is not stupid.*

CHAPTER 3

NOW AND then, after supper, the boy will command the two of them to sit down on the sofa ('Come on, Inés! Come on, Simón!') and enact for them what he calls *un espectáculo*, a show. These are the occasions when they feel closest as a family and when the boy's affection for them expresses itself most clearly.

The songs David sings in his *espectáculos* come from the class in singing he takes with señor Arroyo. Many of them are Arroyo's own compositions, addressed to a *tú* who may well be Arroyo's deceased wife. Inés does not think them appropriate for children, and he tends to share her reservation. Nonetheless, he reflects, it must buoy Arroyo's spirit to hear his creations given body in such a pure young voice as David's.

'Inés, Simón, do you want to hear a mystery song?' says the boy on the evening after Fabricante's visit. And with unusual urgency and force he raises his voice and sings:

In diesem Wetter, in diesem Braus,
nie hätt' ich gesendet das Kind hinaus –

Ja, in diesem Wetter, in diesem Braus,
durft'st Du nicht senden das Kind hinaus!

'Is that all?' says Inés. 'It's very short for a song.'

'I sang it for Juan Sebastián today. I was going to sing another song but when I opened my mouth that one came out. Do you know what it means?'

He repeats the song slowly, articulating the strange words with care.

'I have no idea what it means. What does señor Arroyo say?'

'He doesn't know either. But he said I must not be afraid. He said, if I do not know what it means in this life, I will find out in the next life.'

'Did he consider,' says he, Simón, 'that the song may come not from the next life but from your previous life, the life you had before you stepped on board the big boat and crossed the ocean?'

The boy is silent. That is where the conversation ends, and with it the evening's *espectáculo*. But the next day, when he and David are alone, the boy returns to the subject. 'Who was I, Simón, before I crossed the ocean? Who was I before I began to speak Spanish?'

'I would say, you were the same person you are today, except that you looked different and had another name and spoke another language, all of which was washed away when you crossed the ocean, along with your memories. Nevertheless, to answer the question *Who was I?*, I would say that, in your heart, at your core, you were yourself, your one and only self. Otherwise it would make no sense to say that *you* forgot the language you spoke and so forth. Because who was there to do the forgetting save yourself, the self you guard in your heart? That is how I see it.'

'But I did not forget everything, did I? *In diesem Wetter, in diesem Braus* – I remember it, only I don't remember what it means.'

'Indeed. Or maybe, as señor Arroyo suggests, the words come to you not from your past life but from your next life. In that case it would be inaccurate to say the words come from *memoria*, memory, since we can only remember things that are past. Instead I would call your words *profecía*, foretelling. It would be as if you remember the future.'

'Which do you think it is, Simón, past or future? I think it is future. I think it is from my next life. Can you remember the future?'

'No, alas, I remember nothing at all, past or future. Compared with you, young David, I am a very dull fellow, not exceptional at all, in fact the very opposite of exceptional. I live in the present like an ox. It is a great gift to be able to remember, whether the past or the future, as I am sure señor Arroyo would agree. You should keep a notebook with you so that you can write things down when you remember them, even if they make no sense.'

'Or else I can tell you things that I remember and *you* can write them down.'

'Good idea. I could be your *secretario*, the man who records your secrets. We could make a project of it, you and I. Instead of waiting for things to come into your mind – the mystery song, for instance – we could set aside a few minutes each day, when you wake up in the morning or last thing before you go to sleep, as a time for you to concentrate and try to remember things from the past or the future. Shall we do that?'

The boy is silent.

CHAPTER 4

ON THE Friday of that week, without preamble, David makes his announcement: 'Inés, tomorrow I am going to play proper football. You and Simón must come and watch.'

'Tomorrow? I can't come tomorrow, my dear. Saturday is a busy day at the shop.'

'I am going to play for a proper team. I am going to be number 9. I have to wear a white shirt. You must make a number 9 and sew it on the back.'

One by one the details of the new era, the era of proper football, emerge. At nine o'clock in the morning a van will arrive to pick up the boys from the apartments. The boys must be wearing white shirts with black numbers on their backs, from one to eleven. At ten o'clock sharp, under the name Las Panteras, they will run onto the field to engage with Los Hálcones, the team from the orphanage.

'Who selected your team?' he asks.

'I did.'

'Are you the captain then, the chief?'

'Yes.'

'And who made you captain?'

'All the boys. They want me to be captain. I gave them their numbers.'

The van from the orphanage arrives punctually the next morning, driven by a taciturn man in blue overalls. Not all the boys are ready – they have to send an envoy to rouse Carlitos, who has overslept – and not all are wearing white shirts with black numbers as instructed – indeed, not all have proper football boots. However, thanks to Inés's skill as a seamstress, David has an elegant number 9 on his shirt and looks every inch the captain.

He and Inés see them off, then follow by car: the prospect of her son leading a team of footballers onto the field evidently trumps the business of the shop.

The orphanage is on the far side of the river, in a part of the city he has never had reason to explore. They follow the van across a bridge, through an industrial quarter, then down a narrow, rutted road between a warehouse and a timber yard, to emerge at a surprisingly pleasant site on the riverside: a complex of low sandstone buildings shaded by trees, with a sports field where children of all ages are milling about, clad in the neat dark-blue uniform of the orphanage.

There is a sharp breeze blowing. Inés has the protection of a jacket with a high collar; he, with less foresight, has only a sweater.

'That is Dr Fabricante,' he points out, 'the man in the black shirt and shorts. It seems he will be the referee.'

Dr Fabricante blows on his whistle, one imperious blast after another, and waves his arms. The throng of children scamper off the field, the two teams line up behind him, the orphans spick and span in dark-blue shirts, white shorts, black boots, the boys from the apartments in their miscellany of outfits and footwear.

He is struck at once by the disparity in size between the teams. The children in blue are, simply, much bigger. There is even a girl among them, whom he recognizes from her sturdy thighs and swelling bosom as Maria Prudencia. There are boys too who look distinctly post-pubertal. By comparison the visitors seem puny.

From the kick-off the young *panteras* back away, reluctant to tangle with their heavier opponents. In no time the team in blue has barged its way through and scored its first goal, soon followed by another.

He turns to Inés, annoyed. 'This is not a game of football, it is a slaughter of the innocents!'

The ball falls at the feet of one of the boys from David's team. Wildly he kicks it ahead. Two of his fellows chase after it, but it is trapped by Maria Prudencia, who stands over the ball, daring them to take it from her. They freeze. Contemptuously she side-foots it to a teammate.

The tactics followed by the orphans are simple but effective: they move the ball methodically upfield, shouldering opponents out of the way, until they can push it past the hapless goal-keeper. By the time Dr Fabricante blows his whistle for half-time the score is 10–0. Shivering in the sharp wind, the children from the apartments huddle together and wait for the slaughter to recommence.

Dr Fabricante restarts the game. The ball rebounds off some-one and spins out to David. With the ball at his feet he drifts like

17

a ghost past a first opponent, a second, a third, and taps it into the goal.

A minute later the ball is again fed to him. With ease he rounds the defenders; but then, instead of shooting for goal, he passes the ball to a teammate and watches him loft it over the crossbar.

The game comes to an end. Dispiritedly the boys from the apartments trudge off the field, while the victors are encircled by a joyous crowd.

Dr Fabricante strides over to where they are standing. 'I trust you enjoyed the game. It was a little one-sided – I apologize for that. But it is important for our children to prove themselves against the outside world. Important for their self-esteem.'

'Our boys are hardly the outside world,' replies he, Simón. 'They are just kids who like to kick a football around. If you really want to test your team you should play against stronger opposition. Don't you agree, Inés?'

Inés nods.

He is angry enough not to care if Dr Fabricante takes offence. But no, Fabricante brushes off the rebuke. 'Winning or losing is not everything,' he says. 'What matters is that children participate, do their best, perform to their maximum. However, in certain cases winning does become an important factor. Ours is such a case. Why? Because our children start at a disadvantage. They need to prove to themselves that they can compete with outsiders – compete and prevail. Surely you see that.'

He does not see it at all; but he has no wish to get into an argument. He has not taken to Dr Fabricante, *educador*; he hopes he will never see him again. 'I am freezing,' he says, 'and I am sure the children are freezing too. Where has the driver got to?'

'He will be here in a minute,' says Dr Fabricante. He pauses, addresses Inés: 'Señora, may I have a word with you in private?'

He, Simón, strolls off. The children from the orphanage have taken possession of the field and are busy at their various games, ignoring the vanquished visitors, who wait miserably for the van to arrive and take them home.

The van comes, Las Panteras scramble aboard. They are about to drive off when Inés raps peremptorily on the window: 'David, you are coming with us.'

Reluctantly David extricates himself from the van. 'Can't I go with the others?' he says.

'No,' says Inés grimly.

On the way back, in the car, the cause of her bad mood reveals itself. 'Is it true,' she says, 'that you told Dr Fabricante you want to leave home and live in his orphanage?'

'Yes.'

'Why did you say that?'

'Because I am an orphan. Because you and Simón are not my real parents.'

'Is that what you told him?'

'Yes.'

He, Simón, intervenes. 'Don't get sucked in, Inés. No one is going to take David's stories seriously, least of all a man who runs an orphanage.'

'I want to play for their team,' says the boy.

'You are going to leave home for the sake of football? To play football for the orphanage? Because you are ashamed of your own team, your friends? Is that what you are telling us?'

'Dr Julio says I can play in his team. But I have to be an orphan first. It is the rule.'

'And you said, *Very well, I will repudiate my parents and claim to be an orphan*, all for the sake of football?'

'No, I didn't say that. I said, *Why is it the rule?* And he said, *Because.*'

'Is that all he said: *Because*?'

'He said, if there was no rule everyone would want to play for their team because they are so good.'

'They are not good, they are just big and strong. What else did Dr Fabricante say?'

'I said I am an exception. And he said, if everyone is an exception then rules don't work. He said, life is like a football game, you have to follow the rules. He is like you. He doesn't understand anything.'

'Well, if Dr Fabricante does not understand anything, and if his team is just a bunch of bullies, why do you want to go and live with him in his orphanage? Is it just so that you can play for a winning football team?'

'What is so bad about winning?'

'There is nothing bad about winning. Nor is there anything bad about losing. In fact, as a rule, I would say it is better to be among the losers rather than among people who want to win at all costs.'

'I want to be a winner. I want to win at all costs.'

'You are a child. Your experience is limited. You haven't had a chance to see what happens to people who try to win at all costs.

They turn into bullies and tyrants, most of them.'

'It's not fair! When I say something you don't like, you say I am a child so what I say doesn't count. It only counts if I agree with you. Why must I always agree with you? I don't want to talk like you and I don't want to be like you! I want to be who I want to be!'

What lies behind this outburst? What has Fabricante been saying to the boy? He tries to catch Inés's eye, but her gaze is fixed on the road.

'We are still waiting to hear,' he says. 'Aside from football, why do you want to go to the orphanage?'

'You never listen to me,' says the boy. 'You don't listen so you don't understand. There is no why.'

'So Dr Fabricante does not understand and I do not understand and there is no why. Who is there, besides yourself, who understands? Does Inés understand? Do you understand, Inés?'

Inés does not reply. She is not going to come to his aid.

'In my opinion, young man, you are the one who does not understand,' he presses on. 'You have led a very easy life thus far. Your mother and I have indulged you as no normal child is indulged, because we recognize that you are exceptional. But I begin to wonder whether you appreciate what it means to be exceptional. Contrary to what you suppose, it does not mean that you are free do as you like. It does not mean you can ignore the rules. You like to play football, but if you ignore the rules of football the referee will send you off the field, and rightly so. No one is above the law. There is no such thing as being an exception to every rule. A universal exception is a contradiction in terms. It makes no sense.'

'I told Dr Julio about you and Inés. He knows you are not my real parents.'

'What you tell Dr Julio is of no importance. Dr Julio cannot take you away from us. He does not have the power.'

'He says if people are doing bad things to me then he can give me refuge. Bad things are an exception. If people do bad things to you, you can take refuge in his orphanage, no matter who you are.'

'What do you mean?' says Inés, speaking for the first time. 'Who has been doing bad things to you?'

'Dr Julio says his orphanage is an island of refuge. Anyone who is a victim can come there and he will protect him.'

'Who has been doing bad things to you?' demands Inés again.

The boy is silent.

Inés slows the car, stops at the roadside.

'Answer me, David,' she says. 'Did you tell Dr Julio we have been doing bad things to you?'

'I don't have to answer. If you are a child you don't have to answer.'

He, Simón, speaks. 'I am confused. Did you or did you not tell Dr Julio that Inés and I are doing bad things to you?'

'I don't have to tell.'

'I don't understand. You do not have to tell me or you do not have to tell Dr Julio?'

'I don't have to tell anyone. I can come to his orphanage and he will give me refuge. I don't have to say why. That is his philosophy. There is no why.'

'His philosophy! Do you know what the words mean, *cosas malas*, bad things, what implication they carry, or do you just pick them up like stones and fling them around to hurt people?'

'I don't have to tell. You know.'

Inés breaks in again. 'What is it that Simón knows, David? Has Simón been doing something to you?'

It is as though he has been struck a blow. Out of nothing a rift has opened between Inés and himself.

'Turn the car around, Inés,' he says. 'We have to confront that man. We cannot allow him to pour poison into the child's ears.'

Inés speaks. 'Answer me, David. This is a serious matter. Has Simón been doing things to you?'

'No.'

'No? He has not been doing things to you? Then why are you making these accusations?'

'I am not explaining. A child does not have to explain. You want me to follow rules. That is the rule.'

'If Simón gets out of the car, will you tell me?'

The boy does not reply. He, Simón, gets out of the car. They have reached the bridge that links the south-east quarter of the city to the south-west. He leans over the parapet above the river. A solitary heron, perched on a rock below, ignores him. What a morning! First the travesty of a football game, now this reckless, destructive accusation from the child. *I don't have to tell you what you have done. You know.* What has he done? He has never laid an impure finger on the boy, never entertained an impure thought.

He knocks at the car. Inés turns the window down. 'Can

23

we go back to the orphanage?' he says. 'I need to speak to that odious man.'

'We are having a little talk, David and I,' says Inés. 'I will let you know when we are finished.'

The heron has flown. He clambers down the embankment, kneels, drinks.

Then, from the bridge above, David is waving and calling: 'Simón! What are you doing?'

'Getting a drink of water.' He climbs up. 'David,' he says, 'surely you know this is not true. How can you believe I would ever harm you?'

'Things don't have to be true to be true. All you ever say is: *Is it true? Is it true?* That is why you don't like Don Quixote. You think he isn't true.'

'I do like Don Quixote. I like him even if he is not true. I just don't like him in the same way as you do. But what has Don Quixote to do with all of this – this mess?'

The boy does not answer, but gives him an amused, insolent look.

He gets back into the car, speaks to Inés as calmly as he can. 'Before you do anything rash, reflect on what you have heard. David says that because he is a child he does not have to follow the same standards of truthfulness as other people. So he is free to make up stories – about me, about anyone in the world. Think about that. Think about it and beware. Tomorrow he will be making up stories about you.'

Inés stares straight ahead. 'What do you want me to do?' she says. 'I have wasted a whole morning watching football. I have things to attend to at the shop. David needs to have a warm bath and put on clean clothes. If you want me to drive you back to the orphanage to have it out with Dr Fabricante, say so. But in that case you will have to find your own way home. I am not waiting. So tell me what you want.'

He reflects. 'Let us go home,' he says. 'On Monday I will pay Dr Fabricante a visit.'

CHAPTER 5

FIRST THING on Monday he telephones the orphanage and makes an appointment to see the director. Since Inés is using the car, he has to ride there on the ponderous delivery bicycle, which takes him the best part of an hour, then has to kick his heels in an anteroom under the eye of Fabricante's formidable secretary-gatekeeper.

At last he is ushered into the director's office. Fabricante shakes his hand, offers him a chair. The sunlight that pours in at the window exposes the crow's feet at the corners of Fabricante's eyes; his hair, brushed tightly back, is so unrelievedly black that it may well be dyed. Nevertheless, his figure is trim and radiates a palpable energy.

'Thank you for attending the game,' he begins. 'Our children are unused to spectators. By the nature of things they do not have families to cheer them on. And now, no doubt, you would like to know how it comes about that young David will be joining us.'

'In fact, señor Julio,' he replies, holding himself in check, 'that is not why I am here. I am here to respond to an accusation that has been levelled against me personally, an accusation in which you must have had a hand. You must know what I am alluding to.'

Dr Fabricante leans back, folds his hands under his chin. 'I am sorry it has come to this, señor Simón. But David is not the first child who has come to me for protection, and you are not the first grown man I have had to confront in my role as protector. Go ahead, speak.'

'When you came to the park the other day, you pretended you were there to watch football. But the truth is, you were on the lookout for recruits to this orphanage of yours. You were looking for impressionable children like David who could be sucked into the romance of being an orphan.'

'That is nonsense. Nor is it a romance to be an orphan. Far from it. But proceed.'

'The romance I refer to, which some children find captivating, is that their parents are not their true parents, that their true parents are kings and queens, or gypsies, or circus acrobats. You look for vulnerable children and feed them stories like that. You tell them, if they denounce their parents and run away from home, you will take them in. Why? Why spread such hurtful lies? David has never been abused. He did not even know the word until you came along.'

'You do not have to know the word to suffer the injury,' says Dr Fabricante. 'You can die without knowing the name of what killed you. Angina pectoris. Belladonna.'

He rises. 'I did not come here to have a debate. I came to tell you you will not take David from us. I will fight you every step of the way, and so will his mother.'

27

Dr Fabricante rises too. 'Señor Simón, you are not the first man to come here and threaten me and you will not be the last. But I have certain obligations laid upon me by society, of which the first is to offer a refuge to abused and neglected children. You say that you will fight to keep David. But – correct me if I am wrong – you are not David's natural father, nor is your wife his natural mother. That being so, your standing in the eyes of the law may be precarious. I will say no more.'

After the death, three years ago, of Ana Magdalena, señor Arroyo's second wife, and the scandal that attended it, the Academy went through hard times. Half the students were withdrawn by their parents; the wages of the staff could not be paid. He, Simón, was among a handful of well-wishers who supported señor Arroyo as he battled to save his ship.

If the gossip is to be believed that reaches him via Inés and her colleagues at Modas Modernas, the Academy has weathered the storm and has even, in refashioned form as a school of music, begun to prosper. A core of students, largely from country towns, board on the premises and receive all their schooling there. But the majority of the Academy's students are drawn from the public schools of Estrella, and attend only music classes. Music theory and composition are taught by Arroyo himself; for voice lessons and the various instruments he has brought in specialist teachers. There are still classes in dance, but dance is no longer central to the Academy's mission.

For Arroyo's musicianship he, Simón, has the deepest respect.

If Arroyo is little honoured in Estrella, that is because Estrella is a sleepy provincial city with an exiguous cultural life. As for the Arroyan philosophy of music, which invokes the higher mathematics and treats the music made by human hands as at best a faint echo of the music of the spheres, he has never been able to make sense of it. But at least it is a coherent philosophy, and David has suffered no harm by being exposed to it.

From Dr Fabricante and his orphanage he goes straight to the Academy, to Arroyo's chambers. Arroyo receives him with his usual courtesy, offers him coffee.

'Juan Sebastián, I will be brief,' he says. 'David informs us that he wants to leave home. He has decided he belongs among the world's orphans – the word *huérfano* has always appealed to him. He is being encouraged in this romantic nonsense by a certain Dr Julio Fabricante, who calls himself an educator and runs an orphanage on the east side of the city. Do you happen to know the man?'

'I know of him. He is an advocate of practical education, a foe of book learning, which he openly disparages. He runs a school at his orphanage where children learn the rudiments of reading and writing and figuring before being trained as carpenters or plumbers or pastry-chefs – that sort of thing. What else? He is strong on discipline, character-building, team sports. The orphanage has a choir which wins prizes. Fabricante himself has his admirers on the city council. They see him as a coming man, a man of the future. But I have never met him.'

'Well, Dr Fabricante has gained a hold over David by promising him a place in the orphanage's football team. I come to the point.

If David leaves home and moves into Fabricante's orphanage, he will have to abandon his classes here at the Academy. It is too far to travel back and forth every day; and I don't think Fabricante would permit it anyway.'

Arroyo holds up a hand to interrupt him. 'Before you go on, Simón, let me make a confession. I am well aware of your son's attraction to orphanhood. In fact he has, in an indirect way, asked me to speak to you about it. He says you are unable or unwilling to understand.'

'I freely confess to the crime of not understanding. There is a great deal about David besides his attraction to orphanhood that is obscure to me. To begin with, it is obscure to me why such a difficult-to-understand child was entrusted to a guardian with such weak powers of understanding. I refer to myself, but let me add at once that Inés is as baffled as I am. David would have fared better had he been left with his natural parents. But he has no natural parents. He has only the two of us, deficient as we are: parents by election.'

'You believe his natural parents would have understood him better?'

'At least they would be of the same substance as he, the same blood. Inés and I are just ordinary folk, out of our depth, relying on the bonds of love when clearly love is not enough.'

'So if you and David were of the same blood you would find it easier to understand why he wants to leave home and live among the orphans on the east side – is that what you say?'

Is Arroyo mocking him? 'I am fully aware,' he replies stiffly, 'that it is unfair to demand of a child that he return his parents' love. I am aware too that as he grows up a child may begin to find the embrace of the family suffocating. But David is ten years old. Ten years is an uncommonly early age to want to leave home. Early and vulnerable too. I do not like Dr Fabricante. I do not trust him. He has whispered against me, to David, in a way that I cannot bring myself to repeat. I do not believe he is the right person to direct the moral development of a child. Nor do I believe the children of the orphanage would be good companions for David. I have seen how they play football. They are bullies. They win their games by intimidating their opponents. The younger ones ape the older ones and Dr Fabricante does nothing to check them.'

'So you do not trust Dr Fabricante and you fear his orphans will turn David into a bully and a savage. But consider, what if the reverse were to take place? What if David were to tame Fabricante's savages, turning them into model citizens, gentle, well-behaved, obedient?'

'Don't make fun of me, Juan Sebastián. There are children of fifteen or sixteen at the orphanage, boys and girls – perhaps even older. They are not going to take direction from a ten-year-old. They will misuse him. They will corrupt him.'

'Well, you know this orphanage better than I do – I have never been there. I believe I have reached the limit of my usefulness, Simón. The best advice I can offer is that you sit down with David and discuss the situation in which you find yourselves, not omitting your own position, the position of an abandoned father, full of grief and confusion and perhaps anger too.'

He rises, but Arroyo stops him. 'Simón, let me say one last word. Your son has a sense of duty, of obligation, that is unusual in a ten-year-old. It is part of what makes him exceptional. His reason for wanting to live in the orphanage is not that he finds the idea of being an orphan romantic. You are wrong in that respect. For whatever reason, perhaps no reason at all, he feels a certain duty toward Fabricante's orphans, toward orphans in general, the world's orphans. So at least he tells me, and I believe him.'

'That is what he tells you. Why does he not tell it to me?'

'Because, rightly or wrongly, he feels you will not understand. Will not sympathize.'

CHAPTER 6

SUPPERTIME ARRIVES but there is no sign of David. He, Simón, is about to go in search of the lost sheep when the lost sheep turns up. His shoes are caked with mud, there is mud on his clothes, his shirt is torn.

'What happened to you?' demands Inés. 'We were sick with worry.'

'My bicycle broke,' says the boy. 'I had to walk.'

'Well, have a bath and put on your pyjamas while I warm your food in the oven.'

Over supper they try to elicit more. But the boy wolfs down his food, refusing to speak, then retreats to his room and bangs the door shut.

'What has put him in such a bad temper?' he murmurs to Inés. She shrugs.

When morning comes he visits the shed to inspect the broken bicycle, but there is no bicycle. He knocks at Inés's door. 'David's bicycle is gone,' he says.

'His clothes smell of cigarette smoke,' says Inés. 'Ten years old and he is smoking. I do not like it at all. I have to leave now. When he wakes up, I want you to have a talk to him.'

Gingerly he opens the door to the boy's room. The boy is sprawled on his bed in a dead sleep. There are flecks of mud in his hair, earth under his fingernails. He grips his shoulder, shakes him gently. 'Time to get up,' he whispers. The boy gives a groan and turns away.

He sniffs the discarded clothes in the bathroom. Inés is right: they reek of smoke.

It is past ten o'clock when the boy emerges, rubbing his eyes.

'Can you explain what happened last night?' he, Simón, says. 'Start by explaining where your bicycle is.'

'The wheel got bent, so I couldn't ride it.'

'Where is the bicycle?'

'At the orphanage.'

Thus, a step at a time, a story takes shape. David had ridden to the orphanage to play football. At the orphanage one of the older boys had commandeered his bicycle and ridden it into a ditch, smashing the front wheel. David had abandoned the bicycle and walked home in the dark.

'You went to play football and someone smashed your bike and you walked home. Is that the whole story? Have you told me everything? David, you have never lied to us. Please do not start now. You were smoking. We could smell it on your clothes, Inés and I.'

More of the story emerges. After football the children from the orphanage had made a fire and grilled frogs and fishes that they caught in the river. The older ones, both boys and girls, were smoking cigarettes and drinking wine. He, David, had not smoked or drunk. He did not like wine.

'Do you think it is a good idea for a child of ten to be associating with boys and girls who are much older, who smoke and drink and do goodness knows what else?'

'What else do they do?'

'Never mind. Are your friends here at the apartments not good enough for you? Why do you need to go to the orphanage?'

Up to this point David has responded to his questioning docilely enough. But now he bridles. 'You hate orphans! You think they are bad! You want me to be who *you* think I am, you don't want me to be who *I* think I am.'

'And who do you think you are?'

'I am who I am!'

'You are who you are until a bigger boy takes away your bicycle from you. Then you are just a helpless ten-year-old. I never said the children from the orphanage were bad. There is no such thing as a bad child. Children are all equal, more or less. Except in age. A ten-year-old boy is not equal to a sixteen-year-old boy from an orphanage where rules are so lax that children smoke and drink with impunity.'

'What is impunity?'

'Without being punished. Without being punished by Dr Julio.'

'You hate Dr Julio.'

'I do not hate Dr Julio but I do not like him either. I find him arrogant and vain. Nor do I believe he is a good educator. I think he has motives of his own for wanting you in his orphanage, motives that are not visible to you because you have too little experience of the world.'

'You didn't like Dmitri and now you don't like Dr Julio! You don't like anybody who has a big heart!'

Dmitri! He thought the boy had forgotten Dmitri, the monster who strangled señora Arroyo, was declared insane, and has been locked up ever since.

'Dmitri did not have a big heart, David – far from it. Dmitri was a bad person through and through, with the blackest of hearts. As for Dr Julio, your reasons for wanting to follow him are a complete mystery to me.'

'I don't have reasons and I am not following Dr Julio. I don't have reasons for anything. You are the one who has reasons.'

He gets up from the table. They have been through this argument too often before, he and the boy. He is sick of it. 'Your mother and I have decided you should stop visiting Dr Fabricante's orphanage. That is the end of the story.'

When Inés comes home he delivers his report. 'I had a talk to David. He says he was with some older children who were smoking. He did not smoke himself. I believe him. But I have told him there will be no more visits to the orphanage.'

Inés shakes her head distractedly. 'He should have gone to a normal school from the beginning. Then none of this orphanage business would have happened.'

The normal school that David should have gone to: that is another argument he has been through countless times. He and Inés are into their fifth year together, long enough to have grown bored with each other. Inés is not the kind of woman he would have chosen if he had been free to choose, just as he is not the kind of man she would have chosen if she were interested in men. But she is the boy's mother, in a sense, as he is the boy's father, in a sense, therefore in a sense they cannot part.

As for the boy, he is young and restless. It is hardly surprising that he should be impatient with the routine of life in the apartment block, hardly surprising that he should be ready to abandon home, abandon his parents, and plunge into the exotic new life of an orphan.

How should Inés and he respond: ban all contact with the orphanage or set the boy loose to fly off and have his adventure, in the hope that he will sooner or later return to the nest disillusioned? His inclination is toward the latter course; but can Inés be persuaded to let her son go?

He is woken by a steady knocking at the door. It is six-thirty; the sun is not yet up.

It is the man in blue overalls, the driver from the orphanage. 'Good morning, I have come to pick up the lad.'

'David? You have come to pick up David?'

There is a clatter on the stairway and David himself appears, his satchel on his back, dragging behind him one of Inés's big shopping bags.

'What is going on?' says he, Simón.

'I am going to the orphanage.'

Now Inés appears in her dressing-gown, her hair tousled. 'Why is this man here?' she says.

'I am going to the orphanage,' the boy repeats.

'You are doing no such thing!'

She tries to take the bag from his hands, but he draws away. 'Leave me alone, don't touch me!' he cries. 'You are not my mother!'

He, Simón, addresses the driver. 'You should leave. There has been a misunderstanding. David will not be going to the orphanage.'

'I *will* go!' cries the boy. 'You are not my father! You can't tell me what to do!'

'Leave!' he repeats to the driver. 'We will settle this by ourselves.'

With a shrug the driver leaves.

'Now let us go upstairs and talk this out calmly,' he says.

With a stony face the boy yields up the bag. The three of them climb the stairs to Inés's apartment, where he withdraws to his room and slams the door shut.

Inés tips out the bag on the floor: clothing, shoes, *Don Quixote*, two packets of biscuits, a can of peaches and a can-opener.

'What shall we do?' he says. 'We can't keep him prisoner.'

'Whose side are you on?' says Inés.

'I am on your side. We are together in this.'

'Then find a solution.'

We can't keep him prisoner. Nevertheless, when Inés goes off to work he settles down on the sofa, keeping watch.

He closes his eyes. When he opens them again, the door to the boy's room is open and the boy is gone.

He telephones Inés. 'I fell asleep and David took flight,' he says. 'I'm sorry.'

'You let him run off and now you are sorry? You are always

sorry. A sorry man. Being sorry is not good enough, Simón. Go and fetch him back.'

'I am not going to do that, Inés. It will be futile. His mind is made up. Let him have taste of what life is like in an orphanage. When he has learned his lesson, he will come back.'

There is a long silence.

'This is all your fault, from beginning to end,' says Inés at last. 'You are the one who introduced this man Fabricante into our home. You are the one who is too weak to stand up to the child, who always gives in and lets him have his way. If you refuse to fetch him, if you make me do it, everything is finished between the two of us. Do you understand?'

'I understand what you are saying. I understand that you are upset. But I do not agree with you about David. I think, in this case, we should let him go.'

'Then on your head be it.'

CHAPTER 7

SATURDAY COMES around, and he cycles out to the orphanage in time for the football match. But the grounds of the orphanage are deserted.

In a recreation room he comes upon three girls playing table tennis.

'Is there no football today?' he asks.

'They are playing away,' replies one of the girls.

'Do you know where?'

She shakes her head. 'We don't like football.'

'Do you know a boy named David who joined the orphanage recently?'

The girls exchange glances, giggle. 'Yes, we know him.'

'I am going to write a note which I want you to give to him when he comes back. Can you do that?'

'Yes.'

On a scrap of paper he writes: *I paid a visit this morning in the hope of seeing your team in action, but without luck. I will try again this coming Saturday. Let me know if there is anything you need from home.*

Inés sends her love. Bolívar misses you. Your loving Simón.

Whether Inés truly sends her love he does not know. Since the boy left she has been in a cold fury, refusing to speak to him.

The days pass slowly. He does a lot of dancing alone in his apartment. It elevates him to a pleasantly mindless state; and when he is tired out, he can sleep. *Good for the heart, good for the soul*, he tells himself as he sinks into darkness. *Certainly better than drinking.*

It is the afternoons, the empty afternoons, that are the worst. He takes the dog for walks but avoids the football games in the park and the boys' curious questions (*What has happened to David? When is he coming back?*). Bolívar is getting too old for long walks, so for the most part they settle down together, he and the dog, in the little stone garden around the corner, dozing, killing time.

With David gone, he reflects, *Bolívar is all that is left holding our little family together. Is this what Inés and I are reduced to: being parents to an elderly dog?*

Saturday arrives. Again he cycles to the orphanage. The football game is already on the go. The orphans are pitted against a team in black-and-white-striped shirts that is clearly more skilful and better coached than the ragged band of innocents from the apartment blocks had been. As he joins the cluster of adults watching from the sidelines, three of the black-and-white team perform a slick interpassing manoeuvre that leaves the defenders stranded and nearly issues in a goal.

David, playing on the far wing, looks smart in his blue shirt with the number 9 on the back.

'Who are we playing against?' he enquires of the young man next to him.

41

The young man looks at him oddly. 'Los Halcones. The orphanage team.'

'And the score?'

'No score yet.'

The black-and-whites are adept at keeping possession of the ball. Repeatedly the children from the orphanage challenge and are left floundering. There is an ugly moment when one of the black-and-white players is charged down and sent sprawling. Dr Fabricante, as referee, has stern words for the offender.

Just before the half-time break a black-and-white forward lures the goalkeeper out, then coolly lofts the ball over his head into the goal.

During the break Dr Fabricante gathers the orphans in the middle of the pitch and gives every evidence of instructing them in what strategy to pursue in the second half. It seems odd to him, Simón, that the referee should be acting as coach of one of the teams, but no one else seems to mind.

In the second half David plays on the side of the field where he is standing. He can thus see clearly what follows when for the one and only time the ball reaches the boy in clear space. With ease he spirits himself past one defender, past a second. But then, with the way to the goal open before him, he trips over his own feet and falls flat on his face. Among the spectators there is a ripple of amusement.

The game ends in victory for the black-and-whites. In silence, crestfallen, Los Halcones troop off the field.

He catches up with David as he is about to disappear into the changing room. 'Well played, my boy,' he says. 'Do you have a message for your mother? She is upset, you know, that you do not come home.'

David turns on him a smile that he can only call kindly. 'Thank you for coming, Simón, but you must not come again. You must leave me to do what I have to do.'

CHAPTER 8

THE FEATURE of the orphanage that most puzzles him is its school. Why does Dr Fabricante run an autonomous school when he could easily send his charges to public schools? There cannot be more than two hundred children in the orphanage. It makes no sense to engage teachers and hold classes for so few students, some of them as young as five, some almost old enough to go out into the world – no sense, that is, unless the kind of schooling Fabricante wants for his orphans is radically different from what the public schools offer. Arroyo called Fabricante a foe of book learning. What if he proves to be a foe of *Don Quixote*? Will David submit to being schooled for a life without adventure, a life as a plumber?

Weeks pass without news from the orphanage. At last, exasperated by his inaction, Inés comes knocking at the door. 'This has gone on long enough,' she announces. 'I am going to the orphanage to fetch David. Are you with me or against me?'

'With you, as always,' he replies.

'Then come.'

With no one to direct them, it takes them a while to locate the classrooms, which – they eventually find – are in an isolated building, ranged on two sides of a long corridor open to the skies. Which classroom is David's? He raps on a door at random and enters. The teacher, a young woman, stops in mid-flow and glares at the two of them. 'Yes?' she says.

David is not among the children sitting neatly and quietly at their desks. 'My apologies,' he says. 'Wrong room.'

They knock at a second door, enter what looks like a workshop, with long benches instead of desks and woodworking tools hanging on the walls. The children—all boys—interrupt their respective tasks to stare at the intruders. A man in overalls, evidently the teacher, comes forward. 'May I ask your business?' he says.

'I am sorry to interrupt. We are looking for a boy named David who joined the school recently.'

'We are his parents,' says Inés. 'We have come to fetch him home.'

'This is Las Manos, señora,' says the teacher. 'No one here has parents.'

'David does not belong in Las Manos,' says Inés. 'He belongs at home, with us. Tell me where to find him.'

The teacher shrugs and turns his back on them.

'He is in señora Gabriela's class,' pipes up one of the children. 'The last room on this side.'

'Thank you,' says Inés.

This time it is Inés who pushes the door open, ahead of him. They see David at once, in the middle of the front row, wearing a dark-blue smock like all the other children. He shows no surprise at seeing them.

'Come, David,' says Inés. 'Time to say goodbye to this place. Time to come home.'

David shakes his head. There is a murmur around the room.

The teacher speaks up, señora Gabriela, a woman of middle age. 'Please leave my classroom at once,' she says. 'If you do not leave, I will be forced to call the director.'

'Call your director,' says Inés. 'I would like to tell him to his face what I think of him. Come, David!'

'No,' says the boy.

'Explain to me, David: who are these people?' says señora Gabriela.

'I don't know them,' says the boy.

'That is nonsense,' says Inés. 'We are his parents. Do as you are told, David. Take off that ugly uniform and come.'

The boy does not stir. Inés grips him by the arm and yanks him to his feet.

With a furious motion he shakes himself free. 'Don't touch me, woman!' he shouts, glaring.

'Don't you dare speak to me like that!' says Inés. 'I am your mother!'

'You are not! I am not your child! I am nobody's child! I am an orphan!'

Señora Gabriela interposes herself. 'Señor, señora, that is enough! Please leave at once. You have caused enough of a disturbance. David, sit down, compose yourself. Children, return to your seats.'

There is nothing more to be achieved. 'Come, Inés,' he whispers, and leads her out.

After their ignominious failure to recover the boy, Inés declares she will have nothing more to do with them – with David or with him, Simón. 'From now on I will be leading my own life.' He bows his head in silence and withdraws.

Time passes. Then, early one morning, there is a knock on his door. It is Inés. 'I have had a call from the orphanage. Something has happened to David. He is in the infirmary. They want us to fetch him. Do you want to come? If not, I will go by myself.'

'I will come.'

The infirmary is situated well away from the main buildings. They enter to find David sitting in a wheelchair by the door, fully dressed, his satchel on his lap, looking pale and strained. Inés gives him a kiss on the forehead, which he accepts abstractedly. He, Simón, tries to embrace him but is brushed off.

'What has happened to you?' says Inés.

The boy remains silent.

A nurse materializes. 'Good afternoon, you must be David's guardians, about whom he speaks so much. I am Sister Luisa. David has been through a rough spell, but he has been brave, haven't you, David?'

The boy ignores her.

'What is going on here?' says Inés. 'Why was I not informed?'

Before Sister Luisa can respond, the boy cuts in. 'I want to go. Can we go?'

With Inés stalking angrily ahead, he and Sister Luisa wheel the boy through the grounds past groups of curious children. 'Goodbye, David!' one of them calls.

Inés holds open the door of the car. One on each side, he and Sister Luisa raise the boy to his feet and ease him into the back seat. He yields like a crumpled toy.

He, Simón, turns to face Sister Luisa. 'So that is all? No word of explanation? Is David being sent home because he is not good enough for you, for your institution? Or do you expect us to fix him up and bring him back? What has happened to him? Why can't he walk?'

'I have an infirmary to run all by myself, with no assistance,' says Sister Luisa. 'David is a fine young man and he will soon be well again, but he needs special care and I don't have time for that.'

'And does your director, your Dr Fabricante, know about this, or are you getting rid of David on your own initiative because you are too busy to take care of him? I ask again: what has happened to him?'

'I fell,' says the boy, from the back of the car. 'We were playing football and I fell. That's all.'

'Have you broken a bone?'

'No,' says the boy. 'Can we go now?'

'He has been seen by a doctor,' says Sister Luisa. 'Twice. He has a general inflammation of the joints. The doctor gave him an injection to bring down the swelling but it has not been effective.'

'So this is what your orphanage does to children,' says Inés. 'Does it have a name, this disease for which he was given an injection?'

'It is not a disease, it is an inflammation of the joints,' says Sister Luisa. 'Inflammations are not uncommon among children in the growing phase.'

'That is nonsense,' says Inés. 'I have never heard of a child growing so fast that he can't walk on his own two legs. It is a scandal, what you have done to him.'

Sister Luisa shrugs. It is cold, she wants to get back to the snug infirmary. 'Goodbye, David,' she says, and waves through the window.

Children from the orphanage gather curiously around, wave as they drive off.

'Now you must speak, David,' says Inés. 'Start at the beginning. Tell us what happened.'

'There is nothing to tell. We were in the middle of a game and I fell and I couldn't get up, so they put me in the infirmary. They thought I had broken my leg, but the doctor came and he said it was not broken.'

'Were you in pain?'

'No. The pain comes in the night.'

'And then? Tell me what happened next.'

He, Simón, intervenes. 'That is enough for now, Inés. Tomorrow we will take him to a doctor, a proper doctor, and get a proper diagnosis. After that we will know how to proceed. In the meantime, my boy, I cannot tell you how happy your mother and I are that you are coming home. It will be a new chapter in the book of your life. Who won the football game?'

'Nobody. They scored a goal that was good and we scored a goal that was good and we scored a goal that was not so good.'

'All goals count in football, good or bad. A good goal plus a bad goal is two goals, so you won.'

'I said *and*. I said we scored a good goal *and* we scored a bad goal. *And* isn't the same as *plus*.'

They reach the apartment block. Despite the pain in his back it is left to him to carry the boy upstairs like a sack of potatoes.

In the course of the evening, bit by bit, a fuller account emerges. Even before the fateful game of football, it turns out, there had been premonitions: all of a sudden David's legs would give way and he would find himself sprawling on the ground as if he had been slapped by a giant hand. A moment later his vital forces would return and he could pick himself up.

From the outside it looked as if he had simply tripped over his own feet. But then came the day when he fell and the strength did not flow back into his legs. He had lain on the field, helpless as a beetle, until they had come with a stretcher and carried him away. From that day onward he had been in the infirmary, missing his classes.

Food in the infirmary was horrible: boiled cereal in the morning, soup with toast in the evening. Everyone in the infirmary hated the food and wanted to get out.

His legs were sore all the time. Sister Luisa made him do exercises to strengthen them but the exercises did not help.

The pain was worst at night. Some nights he could not sleep because of the pain.

Sister Luisa had a room of her own next to the ward but she got into a bad temper if she was woken so no one ever called her.

The pain was in his knees but also in his ankles. Sometimes it would lessen the pain if he lay with his knees pressed to his chest.

Dr Julio paid a brief visit every second day because inspecting the infirmary was one of his duties, but never spoke to him, David, because he was cross with him for falling during the football game.

'I am sure that is not true,' says he, Simón. 'I do not happen to like Dr Julio, but I am sure he would not bear a grudge against a child for being ill.'

'I am not ill,' says David. 'There is something wrong with me.'

'Having something wrong with you and being ill are different ways of saying the same thing.'

'They are not the same. Dr Julio does not believe I am a real orphan. He only wants me in his orphanage to play football.'

'I am sure that is not true. But do you still want to be an orphan, now that you have seen what goes on in an orphanage?'

'I am a real orphan. Las Manos is not a real orphanage.'

'It looks pretty real to me. What do you think a real orphanage looks like?'

'I can't say yet. I will recognize it when I see it.'

'Anyway,' says Inés, 'you are home now, where you belong. You have learned your lesson.'

The boy is silent.

'What would you like to eat tonight? Choose anything you wish. This is a big day for all of us.'

'I want mashed potato with peas. And pumpkin with cinnamon. And cocoa. A big mug.'

'Good. I will fry some chicken livers to go with the mashed potato.'

'No. I'm not eating chicken meat any more.'

'Is that what they teach you at the orphanage – that you must not eat chicken meat?'

'I taught myself.'

'You have lost a lot of weight. You need to build up your strength.'

'I don't need strength.'

'We all need our strength. What about some nice fish?'

'No. Fish are alive too.'

'Potatoes are alive. Peas are alive. They are just alive in a different way. If you refuse to eat living things you will waste away and die.'

The boy is silent.

'But this is a great day, so we are not going to quarrel,' says Inés. 'I will make potatoes and peas and carrots. We don't have pumpkin. I will buy pumpkin tomorrow. Now it is time for you to take a bath.'

It has been a long time since he last saw the boy naked, and he is disturbed by what he sees. The boy's hip bones jut out like an old man's. His knee joints are visibly swollen and there is an ugly raw patch on the small of his back.

'What happened to your back?'

'I don't know,' says the boy. 'It is just sore. I am sore all over.'

'You poor child,' he says, and gives him a clumsy hug. 'You poor child! What has happened to you?'

Sobs convulse the boy. 'Why does it have to be me?' he weeps.

'We will see a doctor tomorrow and he will give you medicine that will soon put you right. Now let us have our bath, then a nice supper, then Inés will give you a pill to make you sleep. In the morning everything will look different, I promise.'

Inés gives him not one pill but two, and he does at last fall asleep, curled up on one side with his knees to his chest.

'So he has come home,' he says to Inés. 'Maybe we are not such bad parents after all.'

Inés gives the ghost of a smile. He reaches out and takes her hand, a gesture she for once permits.

CHAPTER 9

THE DOCTOR they see is a paediatrician, a consultant at the city hospital, strongly recommended by Inocencia, one of Inés's colleagues at Modas Modernas ('My little girl used to cough and wheeze all the time, none of the doctors could help her, we were desperate, then we took her to Dr Ribeiro, and she has not had a single episode since then').

Dr Ribeiro turns out to be a plump, balding man in his middle years. He wears glasses with such large frames that his face seems to disappear behind them. He greets Inés and him, Simón, abstractedly: all his attention is given to David.

'Your mother tells me you had an accident while you were playing football,' he says. 'Can you tell me exactly what happened?'

'I fell. It was not only when I was playing football. I fell lots of times, only I didn't tell anyone.'

'You did not tell your parents?'

Now is the time for David to repeat that Inés and he are not his real parents, that he is an orphan alone in the world. But no: facing Dr Ribeiro squarely, he says: 'I did not tell my parents.

They would have worried.'

'Very well. Tell me about the falling. Does it happen only when you are running, or when you are walking too?'

'It happens all the time. It happens when I am lying in bed.'

'And before you fall, when you are about to fall, do you feel you are losing your balance?'

'It feels as if the world is tilting and I am falling off and all the air is going out of me.'

'Does it frighten you when the world tilts?'

'No. I am not frightened of anything.'

'Nothing frightens you? Wild animals? Robbers with guns?'

'No.'

'Then you are a brave boy. When you fall, do you lose consciousness? Do you know what that means – to lose consciousness?'

'I don't lose consciousness. I can see everything that is happening.'

'And how do you feel when you are about to fall, when you are beginning to fall?'

'I feel nice. It is like being drunk. I hear sounds.'

'What sounds do you hear?'

'Singing. And chimes that go clink in the wind.'

'Tell the doctor about your knees,' says Inés – 'about the pain in your knees.'

Dr Ribeiro holds up a cautioning hand. 'We will come to the knees in a minute. First I want to hear more about the falling. When did you fall for the first time? Do you remember?'

'I was in bed. Everything tilted. I had to hold tight so that

I would not fall out of bed.'

'Was this a long time ago?'

'Quite long.'

'All right. Now let us have a look at these knees of yours. Undress and lie down on your back. I will help you. Perhaps your parents can leave the room.'

He and Inés wait on a bench in the corridor. After a while the door opens and Dr Ribeiro beckons them in.

'It is quite a puzzle that young David presents us with,' says Dr Ribeiro. 'You must be wondering whether it is what used to be called the falling sickness. My first inclination is to say no; but that will have to be confirmed by further observation. David's joints are stiff and inflamed – not only the knees but the hips and ankles too. I am not surprised they are painful, and I am not surprised that he sometimes falls. One sees a similar condition in elderly patients. Has there been any recent change in his diet that might be causing this reaction?'

He and Inés glance at each other. 'He has not been having meals at home,' says Inés. 'He has been staying at the orphanage on the river.'

'The orphanage on the river. Perhaps you can put me in contact with this orphanage, so that we can find out whether they have had other cases besides David's.'

'It is called Las Manos,' says he, Simón. 'The person in charge of the infirmary is a certain Sister Luisa. She told us she was not competent to treat David and asked us to take him home. She should be able to tell you what you want to know.'

Dr Ribeiro makes a note on his pad. 'I would like David to

spend a day or two under observation in the city hospital,' he says. 'I will give you a note admitting him. Bring him in tomorrow morning. We will begin by testing his reaction to various foodstuffs. Do you agree, David? Shall we do that?'

'Am I going to be a cripple?'

'Of course not.'

'Are the other children going to catch what I have?'

'No. What you have is not transmissible, not catchable. Now stop worrying, young man. We are going to fix you up. Soon you will be playing football again.'

'And dancing,' says he, Simón. 'David is a great dancer. He is studying dance at the Academy of Music.'

'Indeed,' says Dr Ribeiro. 'So you like to dance?'

The boy ignores the question. 'I am not falling because of foodstuffs,' he says.

'We do not always know what is in the foodstuffs we eat,' says Dr Ribeiro. 'Particularly with canned and preserved foodstuffs.'

'No one else falls. I am the only one who falls.'

Dr Ribeiro glances at his watch. 'I will see you tomorrow, David. Then we can take our investigation further.'

The next morning they deliver David to the city hospital, where they are instructed in the enlightened regime followed in the children's ward: visits are permitted at any hour of the day or night save during the doctors' rounds.

David is assigned to a bed by the window, then whisked off for a first set of tests. He returns hours later looking pleased. 'Dr

Ribeiro is going to give me an injection to make me better,' he announces. 'The injection is going to come from Novilla, by train, in an ice-box.'

'That is good to hear,' says he, Simón. 'But I thought Dr Ribeiro was going to test you for allergies. Has he changed his mind?'

'I've got neuropathy in my legs. The injection is going to kill the neuropathy.'

He speaks the word *neuropatía* confidently, as though he knows what it means. But what does it mean?

He, Simón, slips away and catches the only doctor at hand, the duty doctor. 'Our son says he has been diagnosed with *neuropatía*. Can you tell me what that is?'

The duty doctor is non-committal. '*Neuropatía* is a general neurological condition,' he says. 'It is best that you speak to Dr Ribeiro. He will be able to explain.'

A nurse comes in. 'Doctors' rounds!' she calls out. 'Time for visitors to say their goodbyes!'

David bids them a brisk farewell. They must bring *Don Quixote*, he says. And they must tell Dmitri to come and visit him.

'Dmitri? What makes you think of Dmitri?'

'Don't you know? Dmitri is here in the hospital. The doctors are giving him shocks so that he won't kill anyone again.'

'You certainly will not be seeing Dmitri. If Dmitri is indeed here, he will be in a part of the hospital that is locked off like a prison, with bars over the windows, a part reserved for dangerous people.'

'Dmitri is not dangerous. I want him to visit me.'

Inés is unable to control herself. 'Absolutely not!' she bursts out. 'You are a child! You will have nothing to do with that abominable creature!'

He and Inés stroll in the hospital grounds, waiting for the doctors to finish their rounds, debating this new complication.

'I can't believe we have anything to fear from Dmitri,' he says. 'He is safely locked up in the psychiatric wing. The question is, what if the treatment has succeeded? What if the drugs or the electric shocks have genuinely turned him into a new man? In that case, can we really forbid David to see him?'

'The time has come to be firm with the child, to put an end to his nonsense, both the Dmitri nonsense and the orphanage nonsense,' replies Inés. 'If we don't assert ourselves now we will lose control of him for good. I blame myself. I am going to take more time off from the shop. I have been leaving things to you, and you are too lax, too easy-going. He can twist you around his little finger – I see it every day. He needs a firm hand. He needs to be given direction in his life.'

There is much that he could say in reply, but he holds himself in.

What he would like to say is: *Giving direction to David's life may have been possible when he was six years old; but now it would need a circus master with a pistol and a whip to bring him under control.* What he would like to say further is: *We should face the possibility that you and I were meant to be his parents only for a short while; that we have outlived our usefulness to him; that the time has come for us to release him to go his own way.*

CHAPTER 10

IN HIS office Dr Ribeiro sits them down and briefs them further. The first round of tests suggests that David is suffering not from an allergic reaction – that hypothesis can now be set aside – but from the Saporta syndrome, a neuropathy of the adynamic variety, that is to say, a pathology of the neural pathways along which signals are sent to the limbs. Unfortunately not much is known about the causes of Saporta. It is thought to be of genetic origin. It can exist in a dormant form for years before emerging acutely, as has happened with David. He must ask: Did David exhibit these or similar symptoms in his early years, perhaps as a baby: involuntary muscular contractions, unexplained stabs of pain in the limbs? Is there any history in the family, on either side, of neurological disorders or paralysis? And has he ever needed a blood transfusion? Are they aware that he has a rare blood type?

Inés speaks: 'David is an adopted child. He came to us late. We are not acquainted with his family history. We know nothing about his blood type. His blood has not been tested before now.'

'He is adopted, you say. You have no means of contacting the parents?'

'No.'

Dr Ribeiro makes a note on his pad, then continues. At present David's left side is more severely affected than the right, but Saporta is progressive and if not checked can lead to paralysis. In the very worst case – the worst and rarest – the ability to swallow or breathe may be lost, in which case the patient will die. (He does not use the word *die*: the patient will *lose life functions*, he says.) However, David is a strong, healthy youngster; there is no reason to believe he will not respond to treatment.

Inés speaks. 'How long will he have to stay in hospital?'

Dr Ribeiro taps his lower lip with his pen. 'Señora, we will do our best for the boy. We will monitor his progress closely. In the meantime, he will be put on a regime of physiotherapy to maintain muscle tone and counteract the effects of prolonged bed stay.'

He, Simón: 'David speaks of medicine that is on its way from Novilla.'

'We are in touch with colleagues in Novilla. I will be candid. This is an unusual case. We have not had much experience of Saporta here in Estrella. Should young David be sent to Novilla for treatment? Facilities are certainly better there. So sending him to Novilla remains an option. On the other hand, his family is here – yourselves – his young friends are here, so it is on balance preferable that he stay. For the moment.'

'And the medicine itself?'

'That too has its potential. We are adopting a multi-pronged response to the challenge that David presents. He may have to be here for quite a while. Fortunately we have someone on our staff to help young patients who are missing school. She is quite a livewire. I will introduce you to her.'

'I hope your livewire does not have strange ideas,' says Inés. 'David has had enough of teachers with strange ideas. I want him to be treated like any normal child.'

Dr Ribeiro gives her a quizzical look. 'David is a bright lad,' he says. 'He and I have not had time to chat properly, but even so I can see he is exceptional. I am sure he will get along with señora Devito.'

'David has suffered enough from being treated as an exception, thank you, doctor. A normal schooling – that is all we ask for him. If he wants to be an exception, an artist or a rebel or whatever else is in fashion, he can do so later, when he is grown up.'

Señora Devito is young and so tiny, so fine-boned, that she barely reaches to Inés's shoulder. Her curly blonde hair stands out in a nimbus around her head. She receives them eagerly in her cramped little office, no more than a cupboard really.

'So you are David's parents! He tells me he is an orphan, but you know how children are at that age, full of stories. You have seen Dr Ribeiro, therefore you know David may be with us for quite a while. It is important that we keep his mind active. It is also important that he not lose too much school time, particularly in science and mathematics. It is so easy to fall behind in mathematics and never catch up again. You can be a great help by bringing in David's schoolbooks.'

He glances at Inés. 'There are no schoolbooks to bring,' he says. 'I will not explain why, it is too complicated. Let me simply say that, despite not being an orphan, David has of late been attending classes at Las Manos orphanage. The people who run Las Manos are not great believers in books.'

'My opinion,' says Inés, 'is that he should start his schooling all over again, with ABC and one-two-three, as if his mind were blank, as if he were a baby. He should be drilled in the basics, so that his time in hospital will not be wasted. That is what I would suggest, as a parent.'

They have been in señora Devito's tiny office only a few minutes, but already it feels airless. His head is swimming. 'Do you mind if I open the door?' he says, and opens the door.

Señora Devito's golden locks gleam under the light. 'I will do my best for your son,' she says. 'But I must tell you, even now …' She leans over her narrow desk, bare of everything save a toy bird made of beads and wire, perched on a bar, that stares at them through its little shining black eyes. 'I must tell you …'

'What must you tell us?' he asks.

'I must tell you that at a difficult time like this …' She shakes her head. 'Of course David needs his ABC and so forth. But at a time like this a child needs more than ABC. He needs an arm to lean on.'

She waits, looking at them meaningfully, waiting for her words to sink in.

Inés speaks. 'Señora, during his brief lifetime David has been offered plenty of arms to lean on, all of which he has refused. What he has not been offered is a proper education. It is easy for someone who does not have children of her own – you do not have children, do you?'

'No.'

'It is easy for someone like you to tell us what David needs and does not need. But I know him better than you do, and I tell you that what he needs is to learn his lessons like any normal child. That is all. I have had my say.' She grips her bag and rises. 'Good day.'

He catches up with Inés as she strides down the corridor. She looks magnificent. Self-righteous perhaps, wrongheaded perhaps, belligerent perhaps, but magnificent nonetheless, the woman whom, from the moment he first set eyes on her, he knew to be the true mother for the boy.

'Inés!' he calls.

She stops and wheels on him. 'What is it?' she says. 'How are you planning to undermine me now?'

'I am not planning to undermine you. On the contrary, I want to tell you I am behind you, fully behind you. Where you lead I will follow.'

'Really? Are you sure you don't want to follow the pretty girl you were ogling?'

'It is you I will follow, you I will defer to, and no one else. What more can I say?'

Nearing the children's ward, they hear David's voice, even, confident. 'He knew it was a cage, not a chariot, but he allowed the sorcerer to lock him up anyway,' he is saying. 'Because he knew that whenever he wanted to …'

He and Inés pause in the doorway. Perched at the foot of

David's bed, listening as he speaks, is a young woman, plump as a pigeon, in a nurse's uniform. Around her cluster the other children from the ward.

'He knew that whenever he wanted to, he could escape, because the lock that could defeat him had not been invented. Then the sorcerer gave a crack of the whip, and the two big horses began to pull the cart on which was the cage holding the noble knight. The names of the horses were Ivory and Shadow. Ivory was white and Shadow was black, they were equal in strength, but Ivory was a quiet horse, his mind was elsewhere, he was always thinking, while Shadow was fierce and wayward, which means that he wanted to go his own way, so that sometimes the sorcerer had to use his whip to make him obey. Hello, Inés! Hello, Simón! Are you listening to my story?'

The young nurse jumps up and, ducking her head, scurries guiltily past them.

The children, all dressed in the hospital's sky-blue pyjamas, pay them no attention, but wait impatiently for David to resume. The youngest, a little girl with pigtails, is no older than four or five; the oldest, a sturdy boy, already shows the outline of a moustache.

'They rode and they rode until at last they came to the border of a strange new land. "Here I am going to forsake you, Don Quixote," said the sorcerer. "Beyond lies the realm of the Black Prince, where even I fear to tread. I will leave it to the white horse Ivory and the dark horse Shadow to conduct you further on your adventures." Then the sorcerer gave a last crack of his whip and the two horses set off, drawing Don Quixote in his cage into the unknown land.'

David pauses, staring into the distance.

'And?' pipes up the little girl with pigtails.

'Tomorrow I will see more, and say what happened next to Don Quixote.'

'But nothing bad happened to him, did it?' says the little girl.

'Nothing bad happens to Don Quixote because he is master of his fate,' says David.

'That's good,' says the little girl.

CHAPTER 11

HE IS taking Bolívar for his customary walk in the park when a child comes running up to him, a little boy from one of the upstairs apartments for whom he has always had a fondness – a child crazy about football but still too young to take part in the games. His name is Artemio, but the boys have nicknamed him El Perrito, the puppy.

'Señor, señor!' he calls out. 'Is it true that David is going to die?'

'No, of course not. I have never heard such nonsense. David is in hospital because his knees hurt. As soon as his knees are better he will be back with us playing football. You will see.'

'So he is not going to die?'

'Certainly not. Nobody dies of sore knees. Who told you he was going to die?'

'The other boys. When is he going to come back?'

'I told you: as soon as he is well again.'

'Can I see him in the hospital?'

'The hospital is a long way away. You have to catch a bus to get there. I promise you David will be back soon. Next week, or the week after that.'

He tries to put the encounter with young Artemio out of his mind, but it disturbs him nonetheless. Where could the children have got the idea that David is mortally ill?

Arriving at the children's ward the next morning, he pauses at the door. A man in the white uniform of a hospital orderly is seated on David's bed, his head almost touching the boy's as they peer at something on the bedcover between them. It is only when the man raises his head that he recognizes, with a shock, who it is. It is Dmitri, the man who killed David's teacher, strangled her, who was sentenced by a court of law to be incarcerated for the rest of his natural life – come back now like a malign spirit to haunt the child – and the two of them are playing at dice!

He strides forward. 'Get away from my child!' he cries out.

Smiling pacifically, pocketing the dice, Dmitri takes a step back. The other children in the ward seem stunned; one begins to wail, and a nurse comes running.

'What is this man doing here?' he, Simón, demands. 'Don't you realize who he is?'

'Calm yourself, señor!' says the nurse. 'This man is an orderly. He cleans the rooms.'

'An orderly! He is a convicted murderer! He belongs in the psychiatric wing! How does he come to be here, unattended, among children?'

The young nurse recoils in alarm. 'Is that true?' she whispers, while the child wails even louder.

Dmitri himself speaks. 'Every word this gentleman says is

true, young lady, every word. But consider, before you rush to judgement. Why do you think that the court of law, in its wisdom, consigned me not to one of its many prisons but to this hospital? The answer is obvious. It stares us in the face. So that I could be fixed up. So that I could be cured. Because that is what hospitals are for. And I am cured. I am a new man. Do you want proof?' He reaches into his pocket and proffers a card. 'Dmitri. That is my name.'

The nurse inspects the card, passes it to him. *City of Estrella, Department of Public Health*, he reads. *Employee number 15726 M*. With a photograph of Dmitri, head and shoulders, gazing frankly into the camera.

'I do not believe it,' he whispers. 'Is there someone I can speak to, someone in charge?'

'You can speak to whomever you wish,' says Dmitri, 'but I am who I am. How do you think a man gets rid of the imp that has sat on his shoulder for years whispering bad advice in his ear? By sitting in a solitary cell day and night, being gloomy? No. The answer is, by volunteering for the most menial work, the work that decent folk scorn. That is why I am here. I sweep floors. I scour toilets. And thereby I reform myself. I become a new man. I pay my debt to society. I earn my pardon.'

The old Dmitri, the Dmitri he remembers, was heavily built, overweight. His hair was lank, his clothes smelled of cigarette smoke. The new Dmitri is slimmer, stands erect, smells if anything of hospital disinfectant. His hair, cut short, clings to his scalp in curls. The whites of his eyes, which used to be sallow, gleam with good health. Is it true that Dmitri has become a new man, a reformed man? Evidently so. Yet he doubts it, doubts it profoundly.

The nurse picks up the crying child and tries to comfort her.

He turns on Dmitri. 'Above all keep away from David,' he hisses. 'If I find you with him again I will not be responsible for my actions.'

With a sweet, even submissive, duck of the head, Dmitri picks up his pail and departs.

From his bed David has gazed on the spectacle with an abstracted smile – the spectacle of two grown men fighting over him.

'Why are you unhappy, Simón? Aren't you glad Dmitri found me? Do you know how he did it? He heard me calling. He said he heard me like a radio in his head, telling him to come.'

'That is just the kind of thing a madman says – that he hears voices in his head.'

'He has promised to visit me every day. He says he is cured of his madness, he won't kill people any more.'

Now the young nurse breaks in. 'I am sorry to interrupt, señor,' she says, 'but are you David's father?'

'Yes, I perform those duties as far as I can.'

'In that case,' says the nurse (the nameplate on her breast says Sister Rita), 'could you go to *Administración*? It is urgent.'

'I will go in a minute, be assured'; and then, when she is out of earshot: 'Do you like Sister Rita? Is she good to you?'

'Everyone is good to me. They want me to be happy. They think I am going to die.'

'That is nonsense,' he says firmly. 'No one dies of a sore knee. Let me go and see what the people in *Administración* want.

I will be back.'

Of the two counters at *Administración* he chooses the one served by the older, kindlier-looking woman.

'I have come about a boy named David,' he says, crouching to speak through the hole in the glass. 'I am told there is an urgent matter to be settled.'

The woman hunts through the papers on her desk. 'Yes, I have his forms somewhere … Here they are. There is a consent form to be signed, and an admission form. Are you the father?'

'No, but I act in the father's place. The father is not known. It is a long and complicated story. If it is a signature you need, I will sign anything you put before me.'

'I need the child's identity number.'

'His identity number, if I remember correctly, is 125711N.'

'That is a Novilla number. I need his Estrella number.'

'Can we not use the Novilla number? Surely you don't intend to refuse treatment to a child just because he comes from Novilla.'

'It is for the records,' says the woman. 'When you come again, please bring his Estrella card with his Estrella number.'

'I will do so. You said there was a second form.'

'The consent form. It needs to be signed by the parent or the legal guardian.'

'I will sign as guardian. I have been guarding David most of his life.'

She watches as he signs the form. 'That is all,' she says. 'Don't forget to bring the card.'

Returning to the ward, he finds such a press of bodies around the bed that David himself is hidden: not only Sister Rita and the teacher with the golden curls and the long earrings, señora Devito, but half a dozen boys from the apartment block as well as two children he recognizes from the orphanage: Maria Prudencia and a very tall, thin lad whose name he does not know. Dmitri is there too, leaning against the far wall, eyeing him sardonically.

David speaks: 'The white horse Ivory had a secret power: he could grow wings whenever he wanted. As the cart was about to enter the river, Ivory opened his wings, which were wider than the wings of two eagles, and the cart flew over the water without even getting wet.

'The dark horse Shadow had no wings but he too had a secret power. He could change his substance and become as heavy as stone. Shadow hated Ivory. Everything that Ivory was, Shadow was the opposite. So when he felt the cart flying through the air, he turned to stone, so heavy that the cart soon had to descend back to earth.

'Thus Don Quixote was drawn further and further into the desert by the two galloping horses, the black and the white, until a great wind arose, and clouds of dust covered them, and they could no longer be seen.'

A long pause. Little Artemio, the one they call El Perrito, speaks up: 'And then?'

'They could no longer be seen,' David repeats.

'Did the white horse and the black horse fight?' persists the boy.

'They could no longer be seen,' Maria Prudencia hisses to him. 'Don't you understand?'

'But he comes back,' says the tall boy from the orphanage. 'He has to come back from the desert, otherwise we will never hear the end of his story. We will never hear how he got old and died.'

Maria is silent.

'He did not die,' says Dmitri.

Everyone turns to stare. Dmitri leans easily on his mop, enjoying the attention.

'It is just a story that he died,' he says, 'a story that someone wrote down in a book. It is not true. He disappeared into the storm, on his chariot, drawn by two horses, as David said.'

'But if,' the tall boy struggles, 'if it is not true that he died, if it is just a story, then how do we know there was a storm, how do we know the storm is not a made-up story too?'

'Because David just told us. The chariot, the desert, the storm – all of that comes from David. As for growing old and dying, that comes from a book. Anyone could have made it up. Is that not so, David?'

To his question David gives no reply. He wears the smile that he, Simón, is all too familiar with, the knowing little smile that has always irritated him.

'Will it help if I tell you the full story of Don Quixote?' he hears himself saying. '*Don Quixote* is the name of a book that I found on the shelves of a library in Novilla where we – David and his mother and I – happened to be living at the time. I borrowed the book and gave it to David to read. Instead of returning it to the library as a good citizen would have done, David kept it for himself. He used it to practise his Spanish reading, because, like all of us, he had to master his Spanish ABC. He read the book so many times that it sank into his memory. *Don Quixote* became part of him. Through his voice the book began to speak itself.'

Dmitri interrupts. 'Why are you giving us this recital, Simón? It is of no interest. We want to hear David's story, not yours.'

There is a murmur of agreement from the children.

'Very well,' he says, 'I withdraw. I will shut up.'

David resumes his story. 'There was darkness all around. Then in the distance Don Quixote saw a light. As he drew near he saw it was a burning bush. A voice spoke out of the bush. "The time has come to choose, Don Quixote," said the voice. "You must give yourself either to the white horse Ivory or to the dark horse Shadow."

'"I will go where the dark horse takes me," said Don Quixote boldly.

'At once the bars of the cage that had confined him fell away. The white horse Ivory shook himself free of his traces, unfurled his wings, and flew off into the heavens, never to be seen again, while the dark horse Shadow remained to draw the chariot.'

Again the boy falls silent, a frown on his face.

'What is wrong, David?' asks little Artemio, who seems quite fearless in his questioning.

David pays him no attention.

'Hush,' says Sister Rita. 'David is tired. Come away, children, let David rest.'

The children ignore her. David stares into the distance, still frowning.

'Glory!' says Dmitri. 'Glory, glory, glory!'

'What does that mean, *glory*?' says Artemio.

Dmitri rests his chin on the handle of his mop, devouring David with his gaze.

Something is going on – that is clear to him, Simón – something between Dmitri and David. But what? Is Dmitri reimposing the grip he had on the boy years ago?

With a firmness that takes him by surprise, Sister Rita pushes the children bodily away from the bedside and draws the curtain to. 'That is the end of storytelling for the day,' she says briskly. 'If you want more stories, come back tomorrow. You too, señor Simón.'

CHAPTER 12

WHEN INÉS comes home he has no recourse but to give her the news of Dmitri's re-emergence. 'Like a genie from a bottle,' he tells her. 'A bad genie. The worst.'

Inés picks up her keys. 'Come, Bolívar,' she says.

'Where are you going?'

'If you are too much of a weakling to preserve David from that madman, I certainly am not.'

'Let me come with you.'

'No.'

Though he waits up for her past midnight, she does not return. In the morning he catches the first bus to the hospital. The boy's bed stands empty. A nurse directs him down the corridor to where David has been moved to a room of his own ('Just as a precaution,' she says). Beside the boy's bed, slumped in an armchair, he finds Inés fast asleep, her arms folded on her breast. The boy is sleeping too. Only Bolívar takes note of his arrival.

The boy lies on his side, his knees drawn up to his chin. The frown of concentration has not left his face; or perhaps it is a frown of pain.

He lays a hand on Inés's shoulder. 'Inés, it is me. I will take over now.'

When he first set eyes on Inés, four years ago, she could still pass for a young woman. Her skin was smooth, her eyes luminous, there was a lightness to her step. But the bright morning light exposes cruelly how time has overtaken her. At the corners of her mouth there are drooping lines, in her hair the first streaks of grey. He has never loved Inés as a man loves a woman, but now for the first time he feels pity for her, for a woman to whom motherhood has brought more bitterness than joy.

'*¿Por qué estoy aquí?*' Why am I here? The boy is suddenly awake, staring at him with motionless intensity, whispering.

'You are ill, my boy,' he whispers back. 'You are ill and a hospital is the best place for ill people to get better. You must be patient and do what the doctors and nurses tell you.'

'*¿Pero por qué estoy* aquí*?*' But why am I *here*?

Despite the whispering, Inés has woken.

'I do not understand what you are asking. You are here to be cured. Once you are cured you can go back to living a normal life. They just have to find the right medicine for your illness. You will see.'

'*¿Pero por qué estoy yo aquí?*'

'Why are *you* here? Because you have been unlucky. There were germs floating in the air, and unluckily you were the one they chose to attack. That is all I can say. In every life there are ups and downs. You had good luck in the past, now for a change you have had bad luck. When you recover, when you are well again, you will be the stronger for it.'

The boy stares impassively, waiting for the moralizing to come to an end. '*¿Pero por qué estoy* aquí?' he repeats, as if addressing a dull child, a child who will not learn.

'I don't understand. Here is here.' He waves a hand to encompass not only the room, with its blank white walls and the pot plant on the windowsill, but the hospital and the hospital grounds and beyond them the whole wide world. 'Here is where we are. Here is where we find ourselves. Wherever I am is my here, here for me. Wherever you are is your here, here for you. I cannot explain better than that. Inés, help me. What is he asking me?'

'He is not asking you. He learned long ago that you don't have answers to anything. He is asking all of us. He is making an appeal.'

The voice is not that of Inés. It comes from behind, from Dmitri. Dmitri, in his neat orderly's uniform, stands framed in the doorway, and beside him señora Devito, sparkling with good health, bearing a sheaf of papers.

'Come one step closer and I will call the police,' says Inés. 'I mean it.'

'To hear is to obey, señora,' says Dmitri. 'I have great respect for the police. But your son is not asking you to parse sentences. He is asking why he is here. For what purpose. To what end. He is demanding an answer to the great mystery that confronts us all, down to the humblest microbe.'

He, Simón, speaks. 'I may have no answers, Dmitri, but I am not as stupid as you think. Here is where I find myself. I find myself here, not elsewhere. There is no mystery to it. And there is no why.'

'I had a teacher who used to say that. If we asked her why, and she did not know the answer, she would wave the question away. *There is no why*, she would say. We had no respect for her. A good teacher knows why. Why are we here, David? Tell us.'

The boy struggles to sit up in bed. For the first time it strikes him, Simón, that the illness may actually be serious. Under the blue hospital pyjamas the boy seems pitifully skinny – he who only months ago strode the football field like a young god. His face wears an inward, preoccupied look; he seems hardly to hear them.

'I want to go to the toilet,' he says. 'Inés, can you help me?'

The two are gone a long time.

He addresses the teacher. 'It does not surprise me to find this fellow Dmitri haunting my son, señora. He is like a parasite that attached itself to him long ago and won't loosen its grip. But what are you doing here at this hour?'

'We commence our lessons today, David and I,' she replies. 'We are going to start early so that he can have a rest before his friends arrive.'

'And what will today's lesson be?'

'Certainly not a lesson on how to tell stories, since David is already such an accomplished storyteller. No, today we will revisit the numbers.'

'The numbers? If you mean arithmetic, you are wasting your time. David has a blind spot for arithmetic. For subtraction in particular.'

'Be assured, señor, we will not be doing subtraction.

Subtraction, addition, arithmetic in general, are not relevant to someone facing so profound a crisis in his life. Arithmetic is for people who plan to go out into the world to buy and sell. No, we will be studying the integral numbers, one and two and three and so forth. That is what David and I have settled on. The theory of numbers, things you can do with numbers, and what happens when the numbers come to an end.'

'When the numbers come to an end? I thought it was one of the properties of numbers that there is no end to them.'

'True, but also not true. That is one of the paradoxes we will be confronting: how something can be true but also not true.'

'She is a clever one, isn't she!' says Dmitri. 'So pretty yet so clever.' And he does a surprising thing: he folds the diminutive teacher in his arms and gives her a hug, which she bears with a grimace but without protest. 'True but also not true!'

Is there something going on between the two of them: señora Devito the hospital teacher and Dmitri the mop-bearer?

'You say that David is facing a crisis, señora. How so? David has suffered one or two episodes of neuropathy, but as far as I understand it neuropathy is not a serious disease, in fact not a disease at all but a physical condition. Why use the word *crisis*?'

'Because a hospital, señor, is a serious place. Anyone who finds himself in hospital is facing a crisis, a turning point in his life, otherwise he would not be here. On the other hand, from a certain point of view, each moment of our lives can be said to be a moment of crisis: the path forks before us, we choose the left or we choose the right.'

We choose the left or we choose the right: he has no idea what she means.

The boy reappears, walking stiffly, holding on to Inés. Inés waits pointedly for Dmitri to step out of their way.

'I am going to leave now, *querido*,' says Inés. 'I am needed at the shop. I will take Bolívar with me. Simón will stay and look after you, then I will come back this evening. I will bring you something nice to eat. I know how dull hospital food can be.'

Querido: darling. A long time since he last heard the word from Inés's lips.

'Come, Bolívar,' she says.

The dog, settled under David's bed, makes no move.

'Leave him,' says he, Simón. 'I am sure the hospital people will not mind if he spends the night here. If he makes a mess, it is not the end of the world, Dmitri can clean it up, that is what he is paid for. I will bring him home on the bus.'

He accompanies Inés to the car park. At the car she turns to him. There are tears in her eyes. 'Simón, what is going on with him?' she whispers. 'He spoke to me. He says he feels he is dying, and he is frightened. Is it doing him any good to be here? Don't you think we should take him home where we can look after him properly?'

'We cannot do that, Inés. If we take him home we will never find out what is wrong with him. I know you do not have much faith in these doctors, nor do I, but give them a little more time, they are doing their best. You and I can keep watch over him, make sure that he comes to no harm. I agree, he is frightened, I too can see that, but it is ridiculous to say that he is dying, it is just a story that is circulating among the children, it has no basis.'

Inés fumbles in her bag, brings out a tissue, blows her nose. 'I want you to keep that Dmitri person away from him. And if you see he is getting tired, make the teacher stop.'

'I will, I promise. Go now. I will see you this evening.'

CHAPTER 13

HE FINDS Dr Ribeiro in his office. 'Do you have a minute?' he says. 'It has been a while since we heard from you how David is getting on.'

'Sit down,' says Dr Ribeiro. 'Your son's case is proving to be a difficult one. He is not responding to treatment as well as we would wish, which is a worry to us. I have discussed his case with a colleague in Novilla who specializes in rheumatic disorders, and we have decided on a new set of tests. I will not go into detail, but you told us that David began intensive dancing lessons at an early age, and then more recently there have been sports, football and so on. On that basis we are exploring the hypothesis that the joints, the knees and ankles in particular, have become the site of a reaction.'

'A reaction to what?'

'To too much stress too early in life. We have taken fluid samples, which have gone to the laboratory. I expect a report today or tomorrow at the latest.'

'I see. Is it common for children who are physically active to react in this way?'

'Not common, no. But it is possible. We have to investigate all possibilities.'

'David is in pain much of the time. He has lost weight. He does not look well to me. He is also frightened. Someone, I don't know who, has told him he is going to die.'

'That is absurd. We take our patients' concerns seriously, señor Simón. It would be unprofessional if we did not. But it is absolutely not true that David is in danger. His is a difficult case, as I have said, there may even be an element of the idiopathic in it, but we are applying ourselves. We will solve the mystery. He will be able to go back to his football and his dancing sooner rather than later. You can tell him that, from me.'

'And the falling? His problems did not start with pains in the joints, as you know. They began with falling while he was playing football.'

'The falling is a separate issue. I can be quite definite about that. The falling has a simple neurological cause. We will be in a position to address the spasms that precipitate the falling once his physical health has improved, once the inflammation has subsided and he is no longer in pain. There are various diagnostic possibilities we can explore: some sort of vestibular disturbance that is manifesting as vertigo, for example, or a rarely seen condition known as chorea. But all of that takes time. We cannot hurry the body as it repairs itself. Once the body has repaired itself, we can begin with a course of muscle-strengthening exercises. Now, if you will excuse me ...'

He moons about the hospital grounds, waiting for the lesson

with señora Devito to come to an end so that he can be alone with David.

'How was your lesson?' he asks.

The boy ignores the question. 'Inés rubs my legs,' he says. 'Can you rub my legs too?'

'Of course! Does it help the pain to have your legs rubbed?'

'A little.'

Gingerly the boy stretches out and pushes his trousers down. With cream from the cabinet he massages the thighs and calves, taking care not to press on the swollen knees.

'Inés wants to be good to me, she wants to be my mother, but she can't really, can she?' says the boy.

'Of course she can. She is as devoted to you as only a mother can be.'

'I like her even if she can't be my mother. I like you too, Simón. I like you both.'

'That's good. Inés and I love you and will always watch over you.'

'But you can't stop me from dying, can you?'

'Yes, we can. You will see. Inés and I will be old folks when your time comes, your time of flourishing. You will be a famous dancer by then, or a famous footballer, or a famous mathematician, whatever you choose, maybe all three together. We will be proud of you, you can be sure.'

'When I was young I wanted to be like Don Quixote and rescue people. Do you remember?'

'Of course I remember. Rescuing people is a good ideal to hold before you. Even if you do not rescue people as a profession, as

Don Quixote did, you can rescue them in your spare time, when you are not doing mathematics or playing football.'

'Is that a joke, Simón?'

'Yes, it is a joke.'

'Is mathematics the same as numbers?'

'In a sense. There would be no mathematics if there were no numbers.'

'I think I will just do numbers, not mathematics.'

'Tell me about your lesson with señora Devito.'

'I told her how you dance seven and how you dance nine. But she says that dancing is not important. She says it does not prepare you for life. She says I must learn mathematics because everything grows out of mathematics. She says, if you are very clever you don't need to think in words, you can think in mathematics. She is friends with Dmitri. Do you think Dmitri is going to kill her?'

'Of course not. They would never have let Dmitri out of the locked wing if they thought he was going to kill people. No, Dmitri is a reformed man. Cured and reformed. The doctors have done a good job on him. And they will do a good job on you too, you will see. You must be patient.'

'Dmitri says the doctors don't know what they are talking about.'

'Dmitri knows nothing about medicine. He is just an orderly, a cleaner. Pay no attention to what he says.'

'He says, if I die he will kill himself so that he can follow me. He says I am his king.'

'Dmitri has always been a bit deranged, a bit crazy. I am going to speak to Dr Ribeiro and ask if Dmitri can't be moved to another floor. This morbid talk of his is not good for you.'

'He says that when people die he takes them down to the basement and puts them in the freezer. He says that is his job. Is it true, do you think? Does he really put people in the freezer?'

'That is enough, David. That is enough of morbid talk. Has the rubbing helped?'

'A little.'

'All right, pull up your trousers. I am going to sit with you and hold your hand, and you are going to take a nap so that you will feel nice and fresh when your friends arrive.'

For the next two hours the boy does indeed sleep, on and off. By the time the children arrive he is looking better, with a sparkle in his eyes.

There are fewer visitors than on the previous day, but little Artemio is among them, as well as Maria Prudencia and the tall boy from the orphanage. Maria has brought a posy of wild flowers which she deposits without ceremony on the bed.

He is beginning to like Maria.

'What do you want to hear?' says David. 'Do you want to hear more about Don Quixote?'

'Yes! Don Quixote! Don Quixote!'

'On and on Don Quixote rode, into the storm. The skies were dark and sand swirled all around. A flash of lightning revealed the walls of a castle. Pausing before the battlements, he cried out, "Behold, the bold Don Quixote has arrived! Throw open your gates!"

'Three times he had to cry out, "Don Quixote has arrived!" before with a creaking noise the gates swung open. Mounted on his steed Shadow, Don Quixote entered the castle.

'But no sooner had he entered than the gates swung shut behind him and a voice boomed out: "Welcome, bold Don Quixote, to the Castle of the Lost. I am the Prince of the Desert Lands, and from this day forward you will be my slave!"

'Then minions armed with clubs and staves set upon Don Quixote. Though he defended himself valiantly, he was dragged from his horse, stripped of his armour, and tossed into a dungeon, where he found himself in the company of scores of other unfortunate travellers captured and enslaved by the Prince of the Desert Lands.

'"Are you the renowned Don Quixote?" asked the chief of the slaves.

'"I am he," said Don Quixote.

'"The Don Quixote of whom it is said, *No chains can bind him, no prison can hold him*?"

'"That is indeed so," said Don Quixote.

'"Then liberate us, Don Quixote!" implored the chief of the slaves. "Liberate us from our wretched fate!"

'"Liberate us! Liberate us!" came a chorus of cries from the other slaves.

'"Have no doubt I will liberate you," said Don Quixote. "But have patience. The time and manner of your liberation is still dark to me."

'"Liberate us now!" came the chorus of cries. "We have been patient long enough! If you truly are Don Quixote, liberate us! Make our chains fall away! Make the walls of our prison turn to dust!"

'Then Don Quixote grew angry. "I follow the calling of knight errantry," he said. "I roam the world righting wrongs. I do not perform magic tricks. You demand miracles of me, yet you offer me neither food nor drink. Fie on you!"

'Then the slaves were abashed, and brought forth food and drink, and begged Don Quixote to forgive their churlishness. "Whatsoever you command we will perform, Don Quixote," they said. "Release us from captivity and we will follow you to the ends of the earth."'

David pauses. In silence the children await his next word.

'Now I am tired,' he says. 'Now I am going to stop.'

'Can't you just tell us what happens next?' asks the tall boy. 'Does he liberate the prisoners? Does he escape from the castle?'

'I am tired. All is darkness.' Clasping his knees to his chest, David slides down the bed. His face has taken on a vacant look.

Dmitri steps forward, raising a finger to his lips. 'Time to depart, my young friends. Our master has had a long day, he needs to rest. But what do I have here?' He rummages in his pocket and comes up with a handful of sweets, which he tosses left and right.

'Is David going to get better?' The speaker is little Artemio.

'Of course he is going to get better! Do you think a band of pygmies in white coats can vanquish the valiant David? No: not all the doctors in the world can hold him down. He is a lion, a true lion, our David. Come tomorrow and you will see.' And he chivvies the children down the corridor.

He, Simón, follows. 'Dmitri! Can we have a word? What you said about the doctors – do you not think it is irresponsible to disparage them in front of David? If you are not on their side, whose side are you on?'

'On David's side, of course. On the side of truth. I know these doctors, Simón, with their so-called medical science. Do you think one does not learn a thing or two about doctors, cleaning up the mess they leave behind? Let me tell you, they haven't a clue what is wrong with your son, not the faintest clue. They are making up a story as they go along – making up a story and hoping for the best. But never you mind. David will heal himself. You do not believe me? Come. Come and hear it from his own lips.'

David watches impassively as they return.

'Tell Simón what you told me, young David. Do you have any faith in these doctors? Do you believe they have the power to save you?'

'Yes,' whispers the boy.

'That is very generous of you,' says Dmitri. 'That is not what you told me. But you always were a generous soul, generous and kind and thoughtful. Simón has been worrying about you. He thinks you are going downhill. I told him not to worry. I told him you will heal yourself, despite your doctors. You will heal yourself, won't you, just as I healed myself by casting the badness out of me.'

'I want to see Jeremiah,' says the boy.

'Jeremiah?' says he, Simón.

'He is referring to the lamb Jeremiah,' says Dmitri. 'The lamb they keep in the little menagerie behind the Academy. Jeremiah has grown up, my boy, he has stopped being a lamb and turned into a sheep. You probably had a bite of Jeremiah's hindquarters for supper last night.'

'He did not grow up. He is still there. Simón, can you bring Jeremiah?'

'I will bring Jeremiah. I will go to the Academy, and if Jeremiah is still there I will bring him to you. But if it turns out that Jeremiah is not there, is there some other animal I can bring?'

'Jeremiah is there. I know.'

The seizures commence that same night, during Inés's watch. They start as mere tremors: the boy's body grows rigid, his hands clench, he grits his teeth and grimaces; then the muscles relax and he is himself again. But soon the tremors return, intensifying, following one upon another in a wave. From his throat comes a groan – 'as if something were tearing inside him,' Inés reports. His eyes roll back in their sockets, his back arches, and a full seizure, the first of several, takes hold.

The duty doctor, young and inexperienced, administers an anti-spasmodic, to no effect. The seizures come faster, one upon another, with hardly a break between them.

By the time he relieves Inés, the tempest is over. The boy is unconscious or asleep, though now and then a light tremor runs through his body.

'At least we know now what is wrong,' he says.

Inés regards him blankly.

'At least we know the root of the problem.'

'And what is that?'

'We know what causes the falling. We know what causes the absences, the times when he seems to be elsewhere. Even if he cannot be cured, at least we know what is wrong. Which is better than nothing. Better than not knowing. Go home, Inés. Get some sleep. Forget about the shop. The shop will take care of itself.'

He loosens her hand from the boy's. She does not resist. Then he does something he has not been brave enough to do before: he reaches out, touches her face, kisses her on the forehead. Sobs well up in her; he holds her, letting her cry, letting her grief come forth.

CHAPTER 14

THE FIRST words the boy utters when he opens his eyes are: 'Did you bring Jeremiah?'

'I will tell you about Jeremiah in a minute. First I want to know how you are feeling.'

'There is a taste in my mouth like rotten peaches and my throat is sore. They gave me ice cream but the bad taste came back. They say they are going to suck the old blood out and inject new blood in my veins, then I will be cured. Where is Jeremiah?'

'I am sorry to say Jeremiah is still at the Academy while Alyosha looks for a cage big enough to hold him. If he cannot find a cage he will build one. Then he will bring Jeremiah by bus. He has promised. In the meantime – look! – I have brought you two new friends.'

'What are they?'

'Sparrows. After I spoke to Alyosha I stopped at the pet shop and bought them for you. Do you like them? Their names are Rinci and Dinci. Rinci is a male and Dinci is a female.'

'I don't want them. I want Jeremiah.'

'Jeremiah is on his way. I think you should be more welcoming to your new friends. They have been looking forward all morning to meeting you. Listen to their chirping. What are they saying?'

'They aren't saying anything. They are birds.'

'*The famous David! The famous David!* That is what they are saying, over and over, in their own language. Now what is this about new blood?'

'They are going to send new blood in the train. Dr Ribeiro is going to inject it into me.'

'That's good. That's hopeful. What do you want me to do with Rinci and Dinci?'

'Set them loose.'

'Are you sure? They are pet-shop birds. They are not used to fending for themselves. What if a hawk catches them and eats them up?'

'Set them loose inside where there are no hawks.'

'I will do that, but then you must remember to feed them. I will bring you some birdseed tomorrow. In the meantime you can feed them breadcrumbs.'

It takes a while to persuade the two little birds to leave their cage. Once free, they flit about the room, knocking into things, then finally settle side by side on a curtain rod, looking unhappy.

The story of new blood turns out to be true, or partly true, as he learns from Dr Ribeiro himself. It is the policy of the hospital to keep a supply of blood at hand for each patient admitted, in case it should be needed. Since David's blood is of a rare type, they have had to request it from Novilla.

'You plan to give David a blood transfusion? Is that because of the seizures?'

'No, no, you misunderstand. The blood is a separate issue. The blood needs to be at hand, as a precaution, in case of emergency. That is our general policy.'

'And the blood is on its way?'

'The blood will be on its way as soon as the blood bank in Novilla can find a donor. That may take a while. David's type is, as I said, rare. Exceedingly rare. With regard to the seizures, we have put a new medication regime in place to control them. We will see how it works.'

The new drugs not only leave David drowsy but seem to be lowering his spirits too. The morning's lesson with señora Devito is cancelled. When visitors from the apartments arrive, he, Simón, pleads with them to hush and let the boy sleep. But soon there is a fresh influx: Alyosha, the young teacher from the Academy with whom David has had the closest bond, accompanied by a number of David's classmates. Alyosha bears – triumphantly – a wire cage containing the lamb Jeremiah, or at least the latest in the succession of lambs named Jeremiah.

Once Jeremiah has been released, there is no controlling the children, who run around shouting and laughing, trying to grab hold of him as his hard little hooves skitter and slide on the smooth floor.

He, Simón, keeps a wary eye on the dog in his lair under the bed. Even so, he is slow to act when Bolívar emerges and bears down on the unsuspecting lamb. Only just in time does he hurl himself on the dog, grasp him around the neck, and wrestle him to a standstill.

The huge dog struggles to free himself. 'I can't hold him!' he pants to Alyosha. 'Get the lamb out of here!'

Alyosha corners the bleating lamb and holds him aloft.

He lets go of Bolívar, who now circles Alyosha, waiting for him to tire, waiting to spring.

'Bolívar!' The voice is David's. He sits up in bed, his arm raised, his finger pointing. 'Come!'

In a single easy bound the dog leaps onto the bed and settles there, his eyes locked on David's. Silence falls in the room.

'Give Jeremiah to me!'

Alyosha lowers the lamb from on high and gives him into the arms of David. The lamb ceases to kick and struggle.

For a long while they face each other: the boy cradling the lamb, the dog, panting lightly, still waiting his chance.

The spell is broken by the arrival of Dmitri. 'Hello, children! What is going on? Hello, Alyosha, how are you?'

Sternly Alyosha gestures to Dmitri to be quiet. There has never been any love lost between the two.

'And you, David,' says Dmitri, 'what are you up to?'

'I am teaching Bolívar to be good.'

'The dog is cousin to the wolf, my boy. Didn't you know that? You will never teach Bolívar to be good to little lambs. It is his nature to hunt them down and tear their throats out.'

'Bolívar will listen to me.' He holds out the lamb toward the dog. The lamb struggles in his grip. Bolívar does not stir, his eyes fixed on the boy's.

All of a sudden the boy tires and slumps back in bed. 'Take him, Alyosha,' he says.

Alyosha takes the lamb from him. 'Come, children, say goodbye. It is time for David to rest. Goodbye, David. We will be back tomorrow, with Jeremiah.'

'Leave Jeremiah behind,' orders the boy.

'That is not a good idea, not with Bolívar around. We will bring him back tomorrow, I promise.'

'No. I want him to stay.'

That is how the matter is resolved: with David's will prevailing. Jeremiah is left behind in his wire cage, with a bedding of newspaper to soak up his urine and a bunch of spinach from the kitchen to sustain him.

When Inés arrives for her shift, the lamb is stupidly asleep. She falls asleep herself. When she awakes at first light the cage is lying on its side and nothing is left of the lamb save its head and a bloody tangle of hide and limbs on the once clean floor.

She peers under the bed and is met with a stony glare from the dog. She tiptoes from the room, comes back with a pail and mop, and cleans up the shambles as best she can.

CHAPTER 15

AFTER THE demise of Jeremiah the lamb there is a change in the boy. Visitors are met no longer with a smile but with cool reserve. As for the sparrows Rinci and Dinci, they have disappeared into the bowels of the hospital building. No one speaks of them or of their fate.

One of the nurses, or perhaps señora Devito, has looped a string of festival lights, blue and red, on the wall above David's bed. They wink on and off incongruously, but no one takes them down.

During some of the visits the boy remains silent from beginning to end. On other days he will launch without preamble into one of his stories of Don Quixote, then when it is over withdraw into himself again, as if to reflect further on its meaning.

One of his stories is about Don Quixote and the ball of string.

On a certain day the people brought to Don Quixote a tangled ball of string. *If you are really Don Quixote*, they said, *then you will be able to unravel this ball of string.*

Don Quixote said no word, but brought forth his sword and

with a single stroke smote the ball of string in two. *Woe unto you*, he said, *for doubting me.*

Hearing the story, he, Simón, wonders who 'the people' are who bring Don Quixote the ball of string. Are they meant to be people like him?

Another story concerns Rocinante.

A man came to Don Quixote and said, *Is that the famous counting horse Rocinante? I wish to make it mine. What is its price?*

To him Don Quixote answered: *Rocinante has no price.*

A horse that counts may be rare, said the man, *but it cannot surely be priceless. There is nothing in the world that does not have a price.*

Then Don Quixote said, *O man, you see not the world itself but only the measures in which the world is veiled. Woe unto you, blind one.*

Don Quixote's words left the man puzzled. *Show me at least how the horse counts*, he said.

Then Sancho spoke. *He puts one foot across the other and goes clop-clop for two or clop-clop-clop for three. Now go away and cease to trouble my master.*

Another of David's stories is about Don Quixote and the virgin, *la virgen de Extremadura.*

There was brought before Don Quixote a virgin who had a baby which was fatherless.

Then Don Quixote said to the virgin, *Who is the father of this baby?*

The virgin replied, *I cannot say who the father is because I did sexual intercourse with Ramón and I did sexual intercourse with Remi.*

Then Don Quixote had them bring Ramón and Remi before him. *Which of you is father of this baby?* he demanded.

Ramón and Remi gave no reply, but held their silence.

Then Don Quixote said, *Let a bath be brought full of water*, and they brought a bath full of water. Then Don Quixote unwrapped the baby from its swaddling clothes and laid it in the water. *Let the father of the baby stand forth*, he said.

But neither Ramón nor Remi stood forth.

Then the baby sank under the water and turned blue and died.

Then Don Quixote said to Ramón and Remi, *Woe unto you both*; and to the virgin he said, *Woe unto you too*.

When David's story of the virgin of Extremadura comes to an end the children stand silent, full of puzzlement. He, Simón, wants to protest: *If the girl had had sexual intercourse then she could not have been a virgin*. But no, he bites his tongue and holds his peace.

Yet another of David's stories concerns a scholar of mathematics.

During his travels Don Quixote came upon a concourse of learned men. A scholar of mathematics was demonstrating how the height of a mountain might conveniently be measured. *Plant a stick in the ground that is a yard high*, he said, *and observe its shadow. At the moment when the shadow of the stick is a yard long, measure the shadow of the mountain. And behold, the length of that shadow will tell you the height of the mountain.*

The learned men joined in applauding the scholar for his ingenuity.

Then Don Quixote addressed the scholar. *Vain man!* he said. *Do you not know it is written: Whoever has not climbed the mountain cannot know its height?*

Then Don Quixote rode on his way, disdaining the learned

men, while the learned men laughed into their beards.

'You never told us what happened to the white horse with wings,' says little Artemio, 'the one who flew away into the sky. Did he come back to Don Quixote?'

David does not reply.

'I think he came back,' says Artemio. 'He came back and made friends with Rocinante. Because the one could dance and the other could fly.'

'Hush!' says Dmitri. 'Can you not see that the young master is thinking? Have more respect and hold your tongue while he thinks.'

Dmitri refers more and more to David as *the young master*. It irritates him, Simón.

The death of the lamb has left its mark on Inés too. To the lamb itself she is indifferent. What troubles her is the fact she slumbered through the slaughter. 'What if David had been having one of his seizures?' she says. 'What if he had needed me and I was fast asleep?'

'No human being can work a full day at the shop and then stay awake all night,' he replies. 'Let me take over the night watch.' So they change their routine. When the band of children leaves in the afternoon, he leaves with them. He has his evening meal in his apartment and naps for an hour or two, then catches the last bus back to the hospital to relieve Inés.

Through his influence on the kitchen staff – his powers within the hospital seem limitless – Dmitri has ensured that David gets creamy porridge in the mornings, mashed potatoes with peas in the evenings. 'Nothing is too good for the young master,' he says, hovering over David, watching while he eats, though in fact David eats like a bird.

The nurses all dislike Dmitri, and he, Simón, is not surprised. Sister Rita in particular bridles when he enters the ward, will not respond when he addresses her. Only señora Devito the teacher seems to be on good terms with him. More and more he is convinced there is something going on between them. A shiver runs down his back. What is it that draws her to a man who is a known killer?

He is well aware that Dmitri mocks him behind his back as 'the man of reason', the man whose passions are always under control. *What kind of world would it be if we all submitted to the rule of reason?* Dmitri once asked, and gave the answer himself: *A dull, dull world indeed.* What he, Simón, would like to say is: *Dull perhaps, yet better than a world ruled by passion.*

The drugs the boy is given with his evening meal, meant to suppress the seizures, send him into a deep sleep. In the dead hours of the night he will sometimes wake and give a drowsy smile. 'I am having dreams, Simón,' he will whisper. 'Even with my eyes open I can have dreams.'

'That's good,' he will whisper in turn. 'Go back to sleep now. You can tell me about the dreams in the morning.' And by the blue glow of the night-light he will rest a hand on the boy's forehead until he falls asleep again.

Now and again there is a lucid interval in which they can talk.

'Simón, when I am dead are you and Inés going to make a baby?' the boy murmurs.

'No, of course not. In the first place, you are not going to die.

In the second place, Inés and I do not have that kind of feeling for each other, the kind of feeling out of which babies are born.'

'But you and Inés can do sexual intercourse, can't you?'

'We can, but we do not desire to.'

There is a long silence while the boy reflects. When his voice comes again, it is even fainter. 'Why do I have to be that boy, Simón? I never wanted to be that boy with that name.'

He waits for more, but the boy is asleep again. Laying his head on his arms, he falls into a light sleep himself. Then all of a sudden there is birdsong and the first glow of dawn. He goes to the toilet. When he returns the boy is wide awake, lying with his knees drawn up tight to his chest.

'Simón,' he says, 'am I going to be recognized?'

'Recognized? Recognized as a hero? Of course. But you will first have to do deeds, the kind of deeds that people will remember you for; and those deeds will have to be good ones. You saw how Dmitri tried to become famous by doing a bad deed, and where is Dmitri now? Forgotten. Unrecognized. You will have to do good deeds, and then someone will have to write a book about you describing your many deeds. That is how it usually happens. That is how Don Quixote was recognized. If señor Benengeli had not come along and written a book about his deeds, Don Quixote would just have been a crazy old man riding his horse around the countryside, unrecognized.'

'But who is going to write a book about my deeds? Will you?'

'Yes, I will do so if you want me to. I am not much of a writer but I will do my best.'

'But then you must promise not to understand me. When

you try to understand me it spoils everything. Do you promise?'

'All right, I promise. I will simply tell your story, as far as I know it, without trying to understand it, from the day I met you. I will tell about the boat that brought us here, and how you and I went looking for Inés and found her. I will tell how you went to school in Novilla, and how you were transferred to the school for delinquent children, and how you escaped, and how we all then came to Estrella. I will tell how you went to señor Arroyo's academy and were the best of all dancers. I do not think I will say anything about Dr Fabricante and his orphanage. He is best left out of the story. And then, of course, I will tell of all the deeds you did after you left the hospital, after you were cured. There are sure to be many of those.'

'What will my best deeds be? When I danced, was it a good deed?'

'Yes, when you danced you opened people's eyes to things they had not seen before. So your dancing qualifies as a good deed.'

'But I haven't done very many good deeds in my life, have I? Not as many good deeds as a proper hero.'

'Of course you have! You have saved people, many people. You saved Inés. You saved me. Where would we be without you? Some of your good deeds you did on your own, some you did with the aid of Don Quixote. You lived through the Don's adventures. Don Quixote was you. You were Don Quixote. But, I agree, most of your good deeds are still to come. You will do them after you are cured and come home.'

'And Dmitri? Will you leave Dmitri out of the book too?'

'I don't know. What should I do? You be my guide.'

'I think you should keep Dmitri in. But when I am in the next life I am not going to be that boy any more, and I am not going to be friends with Dmitri. I am going to be a teacher and I am going to have a beard. That is what I have decided. Will I have to go to a school to be a teacher?'

'That depends. If you want to teach dancing, an academy like señor Arroyo's will be better than any school.'

'I don't just want to teach dancing, I want to teach everything.'

'If you want to teach everything you will have to go to lots of schools and study under lots of teachers. I don't think you would enjoy that. Perhaps you should be a wise man instead of a teacher. You don't need to go to school to be a wise man. You can just grow a beard and tell stories; people will sit at your feet and listen.'

The boy ignores the barb. 'What does *confesar* mean?' he asks. 'In the book it says that when he knew he was dying Don Quixote resolved to *confesarse*.'

'Confessing was a custom people used to follow in the old days. I am afraid I know nothing more about it.'

'Is *confesarse* what Dmitri did after he killed Ana Magdalena?'

'Not exactly. You have to be sincere when you confess, whereas Dmitri is never sincere. He tells lies to everyone, including himself.'

'Do I need to confess?'

'You? Of course not. You are a blameless child.'

'And what does *abominar* mean? It says that Don Quixote *abominó* his stories.'

'It means he rejected them. He no longer believed in them. He changed his mind and decided they were bad. Why are you asking me these questions?'

The boy is silent.

'David, Don Quixote lived in olden times, when people were very strict about the stories they allowed. They divided them into good ones and bad ones. Bad stories were stories you were not supposed to listen to because they took you off the path of virtue. You were supposed to abominate them, as Don Quixote did with his stories before he died. But before you decide you are going to abominate your own stories, if that is what you are hinting at, there are three things you should bear in mind. The first is that in our world, which is not as strict as the old world used to be, none of your stories of Don Quixote will count as bad stories. That is my opinion and I am sure your friends will agree. The second thing is that Don Quixote chose to abominate his stories because he was on his deathbed. You are not on your deathbed. On the contrary, you have a long and stirring life before you. And the third thing is that Don Quixote did not really mean it when he said he abominated his stories. He was just saying so to round off his book, the book about him. He was speaking in the spirit of what people call irony, even if he did not use that word. If he had really abominated his stories he would not have encouraged people to write them down in the first place. He would have stayed at home with his horse and his dog, watching the clouds cross the sky, hoping for rain, eating coarse bread and onions for supper. He would never have been recognized, let alone become famous. Whereas you – you have every opportunity to become famous. That is all. I apologize for making such a long speech so early in the day. Thank you for listening to me. I will shut up now.'

The next night they continue their conversation. The boy is

visibly drowsy, but he fights against the drugs, fights to stay awake. 'I am frightened, Simón. When I fall asleep the bad dreams are there, waiting for me. I try to run away but I can't because I can't run any more.'

'Tell me about these bad dreams. Sometimes when we find words for our dreams they lose their power over us.'

'I already told my dreams to the doctor, but it didn't help, they keep coming back.'

'Which doctor was that? Dr Ribeiro?'

'No, the new doctor with the gold tooth. I told him my dreams and he wrote them down in his notebook.'

'Did he make any comment about them?'

'No. He asked me about my mother and my father, my real mother and father. He asked me what I remembered about them.'

'I don't recall any doctor with a gold tooth. Do you know his name?'

'No.'

'I will ask Dr Ribeiro about him. Now you must go to sleep.'

'Simón, what is it like to die?'

'I will answer you, but only on one condition. The condition is that we agree we are not talking about you. You are not going to die. If we talk about dying, we are talking about dying in the abstract. Do you accept my condition?'

'You only say I am not going to die because that is what fathers are supposed to say. But I am not really going to get better, am I?'

'Of course you are! Now: do you accept my condition?'

'Yes.'

'Very well. What is it like to die? As I picture it, you lie looking up into the blue of the sky, feeling sleepier and sleepier. A great peace descends upon you. You close your eyes and are gone. When you wake, you are on a boat skimming across the ocean, with the wind in your face and gulls screaming overhead. Everything feels fresh and new. It is as if you have been born again at that very moment. You have no recollection of any past, no recollection of dying. The world is new, you are new, there is new strength in your limbs. That is what it is like.'

'Will I see Don Quixote in the new life?'

'Of course: Don Quixote will be waiting at the quayside to greet you. When the men in uniform try to stop you and pin a card to your shirt with a new name and a new date of birth, he will say, "Let him pass, *caballeros*. This is *David el famoso*, the famous David, in whom I am well pleased." He will lift you up behind him onto Rocinante, and the pair of you will ride off to do your good deeds. You will have a chance to tell him some of your stories, and he will tell you some of his.'

'But will I have to speak another language?'

'No. Don Quixote speaks Spanish, so you will speak Spanish too.'

'Do you know what I think? I think Don Quixote should come *here* and we should do good deeds *here*.'

'That would be nice. It would certainly give Estrella a shake-up to have Don Quixote in its midst. Unfortunately I do not think it is allowed. It is against the rules to summon people from the next life back into this one.'

'But how do you know? How do you know what is allowed and not allowed?'

108

'I do not know how I know, just as you do not know how you know those funny songs you sing. But that is how I believe the rules work, the rules under which we live.'

'But what if there are no new lives? What if I die and I don't wake up? Who will I be if I don't wake up?'

'What do you mean, *no new lives*?'

'What if the new lives come to an end, and the numbers, and everything else? Who will I be if I just die?'

'Now we are drifting into the language called philosophy, my boy. Are you sure you want to embark on a new language so late at night? Shouldn't you sleep? We can try our hand at philosophy in the morning, when you are more wide-awake.'

'Do I have to take lessons to speak philosophy?'

'No, you can speak philosophy and Spanish at the same time.'

'Then I want to speak philosophy now! What will happen if I don't wake up? And why is Don Quixote not allowed to come here?'

'Don Quixote is allowed to cross the seas and come here, but he has to do so in a book, like the book he arrived in when he came to you. He cannot appear to us as flesh and blood. As for not waking up, if we do not wake up at all, ever, then – nothing, nothing, nothing. That is what I mean by philosophy. Philosophy tells us when there is nothing more to say. Philosophy tells us when to sit with our mind still and our mouth shut. No more questions, no more answers.'

'Do you know what I am going to do, Simón? Just before I die I am going to write down everything about me on a piece of paper and fold it up small and hold it tight in my hand. Then when I wake up in the next life I can read the paper and find out who I am.'

'That is an excellent idea, the best idea I have heard in a long while. Cling to it, do not let it escape. When you are an old old man, many years from now, and the time comes for you to die, remember to write down your story and carry it with you into the next life. Then in the next life you will know who you are and everyone who reads your story will also know who you are. Truly an excellent idea! Just make sure the hand holding the paper does not trail in the water, because, remember, water washes everything away, including writing.

'Now it really is time to sleep, my boy. Close your eyes. Give me your hand. If you wake up and need anything, I will be here.'

'But I don't want to be this boy, Simón! In the next life I want to be me but I don't want to be this boy. Can I do that?'

'The rule says you do not have a choice. The rule says you have to be the one you are and no one else. But you have never obeyed rules, have you? So in the next life I am sure you will manage to be who you want to be. You just have to be strong and decisive about it. Who exactly is this boy whom you do not want to be?'

'This boy.' He gestures toward his body, with its wasted legs.

'It is just bad luck, my boy. As I told you the other day, the air around us is full of malign little creatures, too tiny to be seen with the naked eye, whose sole desire is to creep into us and take up residence in our bodies. In ninety-nine cases out of a hundred they fail to get in. You just happen to be the hundredth case, the bad-luck case. Bad luck is not worth talking about. Now go to sleep.'

CHAPTER 16

THERE IS someone at David's bedside, when he arrives the next day, whom he does not at first recognize: a woman wearing a long dark dress with a collar like a ruff at her throat, her grey hair combed tight against her scalp. Only when he comes closer does he recognize Alma, the third of the three sisters who gave them shelter on their farm when they arrived in Estrella, friendless. So news of David's illness has spread so far!

From the armchair in the corner a man unfolds himself: señor Arroyo, director of the Academy of Music.

He greets Alma, greets Arroyo.

'Juan Sebastián told me David has been ill, so I came to see for myself,' says Alma. 'I have brought some fruit from the farm. Such a long time since we last saw you, David. We have missed you. You must pay us a visit as soon as you are better.'

'I am going to die, so I can't come and visit.'

'I don't think you should die, my boy. It will break too many hearts. It will break my heart, and Simón's, I am sure, and your mother's, and Juan Sebastián's, and that will be just the beginning.

Besides, don't you remember the message you told me about, the important message? If you die, you will not be able to deliver it, and none of us will ever hear what the message was. So I think you should put all your energy into getting better.'

'Simón says I am number one hundred, and number one hundred has to die.'

He, Simón, intervenes. 'I was talking statistics, David. I was talking percentages. Percentages aren't real life. You are not going to die, but even if you were to die it would not be because you are number one hundred or number ninety-nine or any other number.'

David ignores him. 'Simón says, in the next life I can be someone else, I don't have to be this boy and I don't have to have a message.'

'Haven't you enjoyed being this boy?'

'No.'

'If you do not enjoy being this boy, who would you prefer to be, David, in the next life?'

'I would prefer to be normal.'

'What a waste that would be!' She rests a hand on his head. He closes his eyes; his face takes on a look of intense concentration. 'How I wish that in the next life you and I could meet again and go on with these conversations of ours. But, as you say, in the next life we will probably be someone else. What a pity! Well, it is time to say goodbye, I have a bus to catch. Goodbye, young man. I am certainly not going to forget you, not in this life.' She kisses him on the forehead, turns to señor Arroyo. 'Will you play for us now, Juan Sebastián?'

Señor Arroyo brings forth his violin case, briefly tunes his instrument, then begins to play. It is not music that he, Simón, has heard before, but David responds with a smile of pure delight.

The piece comes to an end. Arroyo lowers his bow. 'Is it time for you to dance, David?' he says.

The boy nods.

Arroyo repeats the piece from beginning to end. David's eyes are closed, he is entirely still, in a world of his own.

'So,' says Arroyo. 'Now we will leave you.'

One of his fellow bicycle messengers shows him the newspaper. 'Isn't this your boy?' he says, pointing to a picture of a serious-looking David sitting up in bed with a bunch of flowers in his lap, flanked by children from the orphanage. Standing behind him, presiding over the scene, is señora Devito. Despite the golden curls and the fresh good looks, her image has an eerie quality that he cannot put a finger on.

'Doctors baffled by mystery disease,' runs the headline. He reads further. 'Doctors in the paediatric division of the city hospital are baffled by a mystery disease that has reared its head at Las Manos orphanage. Its symptoms include dramatic weight loss and a wasting away of muscle tissue.

'The case of young David, first to come down with the disease, is complicated by the fact that he has a blood type which doctors describe as extremely rare. Attempts to find matching stocks of blood have thus far been unsuccessful, despite an appeal to collection centres across the land.

'Commenting on the case, Dr Carlos Ribeiro, head of paediatrics, described David as "a brave lad". Although hampered by recent cuts in funding, he said, he and his staff are working night and day to get to the bottom of the mystery illness.

'Dr Ribeiro discounted rumours that the illness is caused by parasites in the Rio Semiluna, which flows through the grounds of Las Manos. "There is no reason to believe this is a parasitic disease," he said. "The children of Las Manos have nothing to fear."

'Approached for comment, Dr Julio Fabricante, director of Las Manos, called David "a keen footballer and a valued member of our community". "His presence among us is sorely missed," he said. "We look forward to a speedy recovery."'

In the aftermath of the report in *La Estrella*, he and Inés are summoned to Dr Ribeiro's office. 'I am as upset as you must be,' he says. 'It is entirely against hospital policy to allow journalists into the wards. I have spoken to señora Devito about it.'

'I could not care less about hospital policies,' says Inés. 'You told the newspaper that David has a mystery disease. Why did you not tell us?'

Dr Ribeiro gestures impatiently. 'There is no such thing in science as a mystery disease. That is just a journalist's embellishment. We have established that David undergoes seizures. What we have not yet established is precisely how the seizures relate to the inflammatory symptoms. But we are working on it.'

'David is convinced he is going to die,' says he, Simón.

'David is used to leading an active life. Now he finds himself confined to bed. If as a result he feels a bit depressed, that is understandable.'

'You mistake him. He is not depressed. There is a voice inside him that tells him he is going to die.'

'I am a medical doctor, señor Simón, not a psychologist. But if you are warning us that David has some sort of death wish, I will take your warning seriously. I will speak to señora Devito about it.'

'Not a death wish, doctor – far from it. David does not wish to die. He sees his death coming and it fills him with grief or regret, I don't know which. Being depressed is not the same thing as being full of grief or regret.'

'Señor Simón, what can I say? David suffers from a neurological condition that brings about seizures – that we have established. During a seizure the brain suffers what we can picture as an electrical short circuit, with ripple effects throughout the entire organism. It should not surprise us if, as a result, he experiences feelings of the kind you call grief or regret, or hears voices such as you describe. He probably experiences many other feelings too, feelings for which our language may not have words. My job is to return him to normal – to a normal life. Once he is out of hospital, in normal surroundings, doing normal things, the voices will disappear, as will the talk of death. Now I must get back to work.' He rises. 'Thank you for coming to see me. I apologize again for the unfortunate article in the newspaper. I take your concerns seriously and will discuss them with señora Devito.'

CHAPTER 17

DAYS PASS. There is no improvement in David's condition. The drugs he takes to ease the pain have taken away his appetite too; he looks more emaciated than ever; he complains of headaches.

One evening, while Inés and he are together at the boy's bedside, señora Devito marches in, followed by Dmitri pushing a wheelchair. 'Come, David,' says the young teacher. 'Time for the astronomy lesson we talked about. Aren't you excited? The sky is beautifully clear for us.'

'I have to go to the toilet first.'

He helps the boy to the toilet and steadies him while he lets loose a thin stream of urine, dark yellow from the drugs.

'David, are you sure you want to have this lesson? You don't have to obey señora Devito, you know. She is not a doctor. You can put it off to another day if you are not in the mood for it.'

The boy shakes his head. 'I have to go. Señora Devito doesn't believe anything I say. I told her about the dark stars, the stars that are not numbers, and she said there are no such things, I am making them up. She has a map of the stars and she says that any star not on her map is *extravagante*. She says I sound *extravagante* too when I talk about the stars. She says it must stop.'

'What must stop?'

'Being *extravagante*.'

'I don't see why you should stop. On the contrary, I think you should be as *extravagante* as you like. You have never spoken to me of dark stars. What are they?'

'Dark stars are stars that are not numbers. The ones that are numbers shine. The dark stars want to be numbers but they can't. They crawl like ants all over the sky but you can't see them because they are dark. Can we go now?'

'Wait. This is interesting. What else have you told the señora that she finds too *extravagante* to be believed?'

Despite his exhausted state, there is a glow of animation about the boy as he speaks of the heavenly bodies. 'I told her about the stars that do shine, the stars that are numbers. I told her why they shine. It is because they are spinning. That is how they make music. And I told her about twin stars. I wanted to tell her everything, but she said I had to stop.'

'What are twin stars?'

'I told you the other day but you weren't listening. Every star has a twin star. The one spins the one way and the other spins the other way. They are not allowed to touch, otherwise they disappear and nothing is left, just emptiness, so they stay far away from each other in different corners of the sky.'

'How fascinating! Why do you think the señora calls all this extravagant?'

'She says stars are made of rock, so they can't shine, they

can only reflect. She says the stars can't be numbers because of mathematics. She says if every star were a number then the universe would be full of rock and there would be no room for us and we wouldn't be able to breathe.'

'And what did you say to that?'

'She says that we can't go and live on the stars because there is no food there and no water, the stars are dead, they are just lumps of rock floating in the sky.'

'If she thinks the stars are just lumps of dead rock, why does she want you to take you out in the night to stare at them?'

'She wants to tell me stories about them. She thinks I am a baby who only understands stories. Can we go now?'

They return. Dmitri lifts the boy into the wheelchair and wheels him out into the corridor. 'Come!' says the teacher. He and Inés follow her down the corridor and out across the lawn, the dog trailing behind.

The sun has gone down, the stars are beginning to emerge.

'Let us begin over there, on the eastern horizon,' says señora Devito. 'Do you see that big red star, David? That is Ira, named after the ancient goddess of fertility. When Ira glows like a coal, it is a sign that rain is on its way. And do you see those seven bright stars to the left, with the four smaller stars in the middle? What do they look like to you? What picture do you see in the sky?'

The boy shakes his head.

'That is the constellation of Urubú Mayor, the great vulture. See how he spreads his wings further and further as night falls? And see his beak there? Each month, when the moon grows dark, Urubú gobbles down as many of the faint little stars around him as he can. But when the moon grows strong again, she makes him vomit them up. And so it has been, month after month, since the beginning of time.

'El Urubú is one of twelve constellations in the night sky. Over there, closer to the horizon, are Los Gemelos, the Twins, and over there is El Trono, the Throne, with its four feet and its high back. Some people say that the constellations control our destiny, depending on where they are in the heavens at the moment when we set foot in this life. So for example if you arrive under the sign of the Twins then the story of your life will be a story of searching for your twin, your destined other. And if you arrive under the sign of La Pizarra, the Slate, your task in life will be to give instruction. I arrived under the sign of La Pizarra. Maybe that is why I became a teacher.'

'I was going to be a teacher before I started dying,' says the boy. 'But I did not arrive under any sign.'

'Each of us arrives under a sign. At every moment in time one or other of the constellations reigns in the heavens. There may be gaps in space but there are no gaps in time – that is one of the rules of the universe.'

'I don't have to be in the universe. I can be an exception.'

Dmitri has been standing silent behind the wheelchair. Now he speaks. 'I warned you, señorita: young David is not like us. He comes from another world, maybe even another star.'

Señora Devito laughs gaily. 'I forgot! I forgot! David is our visitor, our visible visitor from an invisible star!'

'Maybe there aren't twelve constellations in the sky,' says the boy, ignoring the gibe. 'Maybe there is just one constellation, only you can't see it because it is too big.'

'But *you* can see it, can't you?' says Dmitri. 'No matter how big, *you* can see it.'

'Yes, I can see it.'

'And what is it called, young master? What is the name of the one big constellation?'

'It does not have a name. Its name is to come.'

He, Simón, steals a look at Inés. Her lips are pursed, she is frowning in disapproval but says no word.

'Birds have their own maps of the sky with their own constellations,' says señora Devito. 'They use their constellations to navigate. They fly vast distances over featureless oceans, yet always know where they are. Would you like to be a bird, David?'

The boy is silent.

'If you had wings you would no longer have to rely on your legs. You would no longer be in thrall to the earth. You would be free, a free being. Wouldn't you like that?'

'I'm getting cold,' says the boy.

Dmitri takes off his orderly's jacket and drapes it over him. Even in the dim light the mat of dark hair is visible covering Dmitri's chest and shoulders.

'And what about the numbers, David?' says señora Devito. 'Remember, the other day, when we had our lesson on numbers, you were telling us how the stars are numbers, but we did not understand you, not fully. We didn't understand, did we, Dmitri?'

'We strained our intellects but we could not understand, it was beyond us,' says Dmitri.

'Tell us what numbers you see when you look at the stars,'

says señora Devito. 'When you look at Ira, the red star, for example, what number pops into your head?'

The time has come for him, Simón, to intervene. But before he can open his mouth Inés steps forward. 'Do you think I don't see through you, señora?' she hisses. 'You put on a sweet face, you pretend to be so innocent, but all the time you are laughing at the child, you and this man.' She yanks Dmitri's jacket off the boy's shoulders and tosses it furiously away. 'Shame on you!' And with Bolívar by her side she storms away, pushing the wheelchair ahead over the bumpy lawn. In the moonlight he catches a glimpse of the boy. His eyes are closed, his features relaxed, there is a smile of contentment on his lips. He looks like a babe at his mother's breast.

He ought to follow, but he cannot resist an outburst of his own. 'Why mock him, señora?' he demands. 'You too, Dmitri. Why call him *young master* and shout *Glory!* after him? Do you find it amusing to make fun of a child? Have you no human feeling?'

Dmitri is the one who responds. 'Ah, but you mistake me, Simón! Why should I mock young David when it is in his power alone to rescue me from this hellhole? I call him my master because he is my master, as I am his humble servant. It is as simple as that. And what about yourself? Isn't he your master too, and aren't you in a bit of a hellhole of your own, crying out to be rescued? Or have you decided to keep your mouth shut and pedal that bicycle of yours around this godforsaken town until the day you can retire to the old folks' home with your certificate of good conduct and your medal for meritorious service? Living a blameless life won't save you, Simón! What you need, what I need, what Estrella needs, is someone to come along and shake us up with a new vision. Don't you agree, my love?'

'What he says is true, Simón,' says señora Devito. She picks up Dmitri's jacket from where Inés has thrown it ('Put it on, *amor*, you will catch cold!'). 'I can vouch for it. In all the world Dmitri is David's truest follower. He loves him heart and soul.'

She seems to be in earnest, but why should he believe her? She may claim that Dmitri's heart belongs to David, but his own heart tells him that Dmitri is a liar. Which heart is to be trusted: the heart of Dmitri the murderer or the heart of *Simón el Lerdo*, Simón the Dull? Who can say? Without a word he turns away and stumbles back toward the lights of the hospital, where Inés has by now bundled the boy into bed and is busy chafing his icy feet between her hands.

'Please see to it that that woman has no further contact with David,' she commands. 'Otherwise we are removing him from the hospital.'

'Why did you say she was laughing at me?' asks the boy. 'I didn't see her laughing.'

'No, you would not. They laugh at you behind their hands, the two of them.'

'But why?'

'Why? Why? Don't ask me why, child! Because you say strange things! Because they are silly!'

'You can take me home now.'

'Are you telling me you want to come home?'

'Yes. Bolívar too. Bolívar doesn't like it here.'

'Then let us go at once. Simón, wrap him in a blanket.'

The way out, however, is blocked by señora Devito, with Dmitri flanking her. 'What is going on here?' she demands with a frown.

'Simón and Inés are taking me away,' says David. 'They are going to let me die at home.'

'You are a patient here. You may not leave unless you are signed out by a doctor.'

'Then call a doctor!' says Inés. 'At once!'

'I will call the duty doctor. But I warn you: it is up to the doctor and to him alone to say whether David may leave.'

'Are you sure you want to leave us, young man?' says Dmitri. 'We will be desolate without you. You bring life to this joyless place. And think of your friends. When they arrive tomorrow, expecting to see you, expecting to sit at your feet, your room will stand empty, you will be gone. What will I say to them? *The young master has fled? The young master has abandoned you?* Their hearts will be broken.'

'They can come to our apartment,' says the boy.

'And what about me? What about old Dmitri? Will Dmitri be welcome in señora Inés's fine apartment? And the pretty señorita, your teacher – will she be welcome?'

Señora Devito returns with a harried-looking young man at her side.

'This is the boy,' says señora Devito, 'the one with the so-called mystery illness. And these are Inés and Simón.'

'You are the parents?' says the young doctor.

'No,' says he, Simón. 'We are – '

'Yes,' says Inés, 'we are the parents.'

'And who is in charge of the case?'

'Dr Ribeiro,' says señora Devito.

'I am sorry, but I cannot sign a release until I have Dr Ribeiro's authorization.'

Inés draws herself up. 'I do not need authorization from anyone to take my child home.'

'I don't have a mystery illness,' says the boy. 'I am number one hundred. One hundred is not a mystery number. Number one hundred is the number that has to die.'

The doctor regards him crossly. 'That is not how statistics work, young man. You are not going to die. This is a hospital. We do not let children die here.' He turns to Inés. 'Come back tomorrow and speak to Dr Ribeiro. I will leave a note for him.' He turns to Dmitri. 'Take our young friend back to the ward, please. And what is the dog doing here? You know that animals are not allowed.'

Inés does not deign to argue. Gripping the handles of the wheelchair, she pushes past the doctor.

Dmitri bars her way. 'A mother's love,' he says. 'It is a privilege to see it, it stirs the heart. Truly. But we cannot let you remove our young master.'

As he reaches out to take the wheelchair, a low growl comes from Bolívar. Dmitri withdraws the offending hand but continues to block Inés's way. The dog growls again, deep in his throat. His ears are flattened, his upper lip drawn back to reveal long, yellowing teeth.

'Out of the way, Dmitri,' says he, Simón.

The dog takes a first slow step toward Dmitri, a second. Dmitri stands his ground.

'Bolívar, be still!' commands the boy.

The dog halts, his gaze still fixed on Dmitri.

'Dmitri, give way!' says the boy.

Dmitri gives way.

The young doctor addresses Dmitri. 'Who was it who allowed this dangerous animal onto the premises? Was it you?'

'He is not a dangerous animal,' says the boy. 'He is my guardian. He is guarding me.'

Without a hand being laid on them they depart the hospital. He, Simón, lifts the boy into the back seat of Inés's car; the dog leaps in; they abandon the wheelchair in the car park.

He turns to Inés. 'Inés, you were magnificent.' It is true: never has she been more resolute, more commanding, more queenly.

'Bolívar was magnificent too,' says the boy. 'Bolívar is king of the dogs. Are we going to be a family again?'

'Yes,' says he, Simón, 'we are going to be a family again.'

CHAPTER 18

AT AROUND midnight that same night a new round of seizures commences, coming one after another with barely a break. At his wits' end, he, Simón, drives to the hospital and pleads with the night nurse for the boy's medicines. She refuses. 'The way you are acting is nothing short of criminal,' she says. 'You should never have been allowed to remove the child. You have no conception of how serious his condition is. Give me your address. I am going to send an ambulance at once.'

Two hours later the boy is back in his bed in the hospital, in a deep, drugged sleep.

Dr Ribeiro, when told what went on during the night, is cold in his anger. 'I can have you barred from the hospital,' he says. 'Even if you were the child's parents, which you are not, I could have you barred, you and that savage dog of yours. What kind of people are you?'

He and Inés stand mute.

'Please leave now,' says Dr Ribeiro. 'Go home. The staff will give you a call when the child is stable again.'

'He won't eat,' says Inés. 'He looks like a skeleton.'

'We will take care of that, don't worry.'

'He says he is not hungry. He says he does not need food any more. I don't understand what is coming over him. It frightens me.'

'We will take care of it. Go home now.'

The next day Inés receives a call from Sister Rita. 'David is asking for you,' says Sister Rita. 'For you and your husband. Dr Ribeiro agrees that you can visit, but only for a few minutes, and not the dog. The dog is forbidden.'

Even after two days the change in David is striking. He seems to have shrunk, as if he were a six-year-old again. His face is pale and drawn. His lips move but they can make out no word. There is a helpless appeal in his look.

'Bolívar,' he croaks.

'Bolívar is at home,' says he, Simón. 'He is resting. He is recuperating his forces. He will come and see you soon.'

'My book,' croaks the boy.

He goes in search of Sister Rita. 'He is asking for his Don Quixote book. I have hunted for it but I can't find it anywhere.'

'I am busy now. I will look for it later,' says Sister Rita. There is a new coldness in her tone.

'I am sorry about what happened last night,' he says. 'We did not think.'

'Being sorry does not help,' says Sister Rita. 'Keeping out of the way would help. Letting us do our work. Accepting that we are doing whatever is humanly possible to save David.'

'We do not seem to be popular here, you and I,' he tells Inés.

'Why don't you go back to the shop. I will stay on.'

He tries to buy a sandwich in the canteen but is refused ('Sorry, staff only.').

When the faithful core of David's young friends arrive in the afternoon, they are turned away by Sister Rita. 'David is too tired for visitors. Come back tomorrow.'

At the end of the day he waylays Sister Rita on her way out. 'Did you find the book?' She gives him an uncomprehending stare. '*Don Quixote*. David's book. Did you find it?'

'I will look for it when I have time,' she says.

He hangs around in the corridor, his stomach growling with hunger. After the boy has been given his medication and settled down for the night, he slips in quietly and, stretched out on the armchair, falls asleep.

He is woken by an insistent whispering: 'Simón! Simón!'

At once he is alert.

'I have remembered another song, Simón, only I can't sing it, my throat is too sore.'

He helps the boy to drink.

'The red pills make me dizzy,' he says. 'Do I have to take them? It is like bees buzzing in my head, zzz-zzz-zzz. Simón, in the next life will I do sexual intercourse?'

'You will have sexual intercourse in this life, when you are old enough, and you will have it in the next life too, and all the lives after that – that I can promise you.'

'When I was small I didn't know what sexual intercourse was, but now I know. And Simón, when is the blood going to come?'

'The new blood? Sometime today, or tomorrow at the latest.'

128

'That's good. Do you know what Dmitri says? He says, when they inject the new blood into me my sickness will fall away and I will stand up in all my glory. What is my glory?'

'Glory is a kind of light that shines out of people who are very strong and very healthy, like athletes and dancers. Football players too.'

'But Simón, why did you hide me in the cupboard?'

'When did I hide you in a cupboard? I don't remember doing any such thing.'

'Yes, you did! When I was small, some people came in the night, and you locked me in a cupboard and told them you didn't have any children. Don't you remember?'

'Ah, I remember now! Those people who came in the night were census-takers. I hid you in the cupboard so that they would not turn you into a number and put you on their census list.'

'You didn't want me to give them my message.'

'That is not true. It was for your own sake that I hid you, to save you from the census. What was the message you were going to give them?'

'My message. Simón, how do you say *aquí* in another language?'

'I don't know, my boy, I am not good at languages. I told you before: *aquí* is just *aquí*. It is the same no matter what language you speak. Here is here.'

'But how do you say *aquí* in other words?'

'I don't know any other words for it. Everyone understands where here is. Why do you want other words?'

'I want to know why I am here.'

'You are here to bring light into our lives, my boy, into Inés's

129

life and my life and the lives of all the people who meet you.'

'And Bolívar's life too.'

'And Bolívar too. That is why you are here. It is as simple as that.'

The boy does not seem to hear. His eyes are closed, as if he is listening to a far-off voice.

'Simón, I am falling,' he whispers.

'You are not falling. I am holding you. It is just dizziness. It will wear off.'

Slowly the boy returns from wherever he has been.

'Simón,' he says, 'there is a dream, always the same dream. I keep going back into it. I am in the cupboard and I can't breathe and I can't get out. The dream won't go away. It is waiting for me to come.'

'I am sorry. From my heart I apologize. I did not realize hiding you from those people would leave such bad memories behind. If it is any consolation, señor Arroyo hid his sons too, Joaquín and Damián, to prevent them from being turned into numbers. What was the message you would have given the census-takers if I had not hidden you in the cupboard?'

The boy shakes his head. 'It is not yet time.'

'It is not yet time for your message? It is not yet time for me to hear it? What do you mean? When will it be time?'

The boy is silent.

No sooner has Sister Rita arrived on duty than he is chased peremptorily out of David's room. 'Did you not hear what Dr

Ribeiro said, señor? You are not good for the boy! Go home! Stop interfering!'

He catches the bus to the city centre, has a huge breakfast, drops in on Inés at Modas Modernas. They sit together in her office at the back of the shop. 'I spent the night with David,' he says. 'He is looking worse than ever. The drugs are sapping his strength. He wanted to sing to me – he has a new song – but he could not, he was too weak. He talks about blood all the time, the blood that is going to arrive by train and save him. His hopes are pinned on that.'

'What are you going to do?' says Inés.

'I don't know, my dear, I don't know. I am quite desperate.'

Querida. He has never called her that before.

'I am going to see a new doctor this afternoon,' she says. 'Not one of the hospital doctors. Someone independent. Inocencia recommends him. She says he cured the child of one of her neighbours when the regular doctors had given up. I want him to go to the hospital and examine David. I don't have faith in Dr Ribeiro any more.'

'Would you like me to come with you?'

'No. You will just complicate things.'

'Is that what I do – complicate things?'

She is silent.

'Well,' he says, 'I hope this independent doctor is a real doctor with real credentials, otherwise they will not allow him near David.'

Inés stands up. 'Why must you be so negative, Simón? What is more important: that David be cured or that we follow the rules and regulations of that hospital of theirs?'

He bows his head, takes his leave.

CHAPTER 19

BECAUSE THE hospital has criteria of its own for determining who should be contacted in an emergency, he and Inés are not summoned to David's bedside when his heartbeat grows irregular and his breathing laboured and the doctors begin to prepare for the worst. Instead a call is put through to the office of Dr Fabricante at the orphanage, and from there to Sister Luisa in the infirmary. Sister Luisa is busy attending to a boy with ringworm; by the time she arrives at the hospital, David has already been declared dead, the cause of death yet to be settled; the room where he died is closed until further notice (so says the sign on the door) to all but authorized personnel.

Sister Luisa is asked to sign a declaration accepting responsibility for funerary arrangements. Prudently she refuses to do so before she has consulted her superior, Dr Fabricante.

When he, Simón, arrives in the afternoon, he is confronted with the same printed sign: CLOSED UNTIL FURTHER NOTICE. He tries the handle, but the door is locked. He enquires at the information desk: *Where is my son?* The woman at the desk pretends not to know. *He must have been moved*: that is all she is prepared to say.

He returns to the room, kicks at the door until the lock breaks. The bed is empty, the room is deserted, there is a smell of disinfectant in the air.

'He is not here,' says Dmitri's voice behind him. 'And on top of that you will have to pay for the damage to the door.'

'Where is he?'

'Do you want to see? I will show you.'

Down a flight of steps Dmitri leads him, to the basement, then down a corridor cluttered with carton boxes and cast-off equipment. From the ring of keys at his belt he selects one and unlocks a door marked N-5. David is lying naked on a padded table, the kind of table used for ironing laundry, with at his head the string of festive lights flashing alternately red and blue, and at his feet a bunch of lilies. The emaciated limbs, with their swollen joints, look less grotesque in death than in life.

'I brought the lights along,' says Dmitri. 'It seemed appropriate. The flowers come from the orphanage.'

It is as if the air is being sucked from his lungs. *It is a show*, he thinks, but he can feel the panic behind the thinking. *If I go along with the show*, he thinks, *if I pretend it is real, then it will come to an end and David will sit up and smile, and all will be as it was before. But above all*, he thinks, *Inés must not hear of this, Inés must be protected, otherwise she will be destroyed, destroyed!*

'Take the lights away,' he says.

Dmitri does not stir.

'How did it happen?' he says. There is no air in the room, he can barely hear his own voice.

'He is departed, as you can see,' says Dmitri. 'The organs of the body could not hold out any longer, poor child. But in a deeper sense he is not departed. In a deeper sense he is still with us. That is what I believe. I am sure you feel the same way.'

'Do not try to tell me about my child,' he whispers.

'Not your child, Simón. He belonged to all of us.'

'Go away. Leave me with him.'

'I cannot do that, Simón. I have to lock up. That is the rule. But take your time. Say your goodbyes. I will wait.'

He forces himself to look at the corpse: at the wasted limbs, whose extremities are already turning blue, at the slack, empty hands, at the shrivelled, never-used sex, at the face closed as if in concentration. He touches the cheek, unnaturally cold. He presses his lips to the forehead. After which, without knowing how or why, he finds himself on his hands and knees on the floor.

Let it all come to an end, he thinks. *Let me wake and let it be at an end. Or let me not wake, ever.*

'Take your time,' says Dmitri. 'It is difficult, I know.'

From the lobby he telephones Modas Modernas. Inocencia answers. His voice is not his own, he has to struggle to make himself heard. 'Simón here,' he says. 'Tell Inés to come to the hospital. Tell her to come at once. Say I will meet her in the car park.'

From his face, from his bearing, Inés sees in a flash what has happened. 'No!' she cries. 'No, no, no! Why didn't you tell me?'

'Be calm, Inés. Be strong. Give me your arm. Let us face this together.'

Dmitri is lounging in the corridor, keeping an eye out for them. 'So sorry,' he murmurs. Inés refuses to acknowledge him. 'Follow me,' says Dmitri, and marches briskly ahead.

The coloured lights have not been removed. Inés sweeps them to the floor, and the lilies too: there is a pop as one of the bulbs bursts. She tries to lift the dead child in her arms; his head lolls to one side.

'I will be waiting outside,' says Dmitri. 'I will let you two do your grieving in peace.'

'How did it happen?' says Inés. 'Why didn't you call me?'

'They kept it from me. They kept it from both of us. Believe me, I telephoned as soon as I found out.'

'So he was all alone?' says Inés. She releases the crumpled body onto the table, presses the feet together, folds the limp hands. 'He was all alone? Where were you?'

Where was he? He cannot bear to think. At the moment when the child gave up the ghost, was he absent, inattentive, deep in sleep?

'I asked to speak to Dr Ribeiro, but it turns out he is not available,' he says. 'No one is available. They do not want to face us. They are in hiding, waiting for us to go away.'

Coming up out of the basement, he glimpses the retreating figure of señora Devito. Spurred on by anger he sprints after her. 'Señora!' he calls. 'May I speak to you?'

She appears not to hear. Only when he grips her by the arm does she turn toward him, frowning. 'Yes? What is it?'

'I don't know whether you are aware, señora, but my son passed away this morning. His mother and I were not with him at the end. He died all alone. Why were we not there, you may ask? Because we were not called.'

'Yes? It is not my responsibility to call in the family members.'

'No, it is not your responsibility. Nothing is your responsibility. Your friend Dmitri locks the poor child away from us but that is not your responsibility either. Yet you took him out into the cold, the other night, for the sake of an astronomy lesson, of all things. Why? Why did you feel it your responsibility to teach a sick child the stupid names of the stars?'

'Calm yourself, señor! David did not die because of a touch of night air. You and your wife, on the other hand, removed him by force from our care, against his will and against all advice. Who do you think is to blame for what followed?'

'Against his will? David wanted desperately to get out of your clutches and come home.'

'Sit down, señor. Listen to me. It is time for you to hear the truth, unpleasant though it may be. I knew David. I was his teacher and his friend. He trusted me. We spent hours together while he poured out his heart to me. David was a deeply conflicted child. He did *not* want to go back to what you call his home. On the contrary, he wanted to work himself free of you and your wife. He complained that you in particular were stifling him, that you would not let him grow up to be the person he wanted to be. If he did not say so to your face, it was because he was reluctant to hurt you. Should we be surprised if all this inner conflict began to manifest itself at a physical level? No. In its pain and contortion his body was giving expression to the dilemma he confronted, a dilemma he found literally unbearable.'

'What nonsense! You were never David's friend! He put up with your lessons only because he was trapped in bed, unable to get away. As for your diagnosis of his illness, it is simply laughable.'

'It is not just my diagnosis. At my recommendation, David had a number of sessions with a psychiatric specialist, and would have had more if his condition had not deteriorated. That specialist supports my reading of David to the hilt. As for astronomy, it is my job to keep the intellectual interests of our children alive. David and I often exchanged ideas about the stars and the comets and so forth.'

'Exchanged ideas! You pooh-poohed his stories about the stars. You called them *extravagantes*. You told him the stars have nothing to do with numbers, they are simply lumps of rock floating in space. What kind of teacher are you to destroy a child's illusions like that?'

'Stars are indeed lumps of rock, señor. Numbers, in contrast, are a human invention. Numbers have nothing to do with stars. Nothing. We created the numbers out of thin air so that we could use when we calculate weights and measures. But all of that is beside the point. David told me his stories and I told him mine. His stories, which he had evidently been fed in the music academy, struck me as abstract and bloodless. The stories I told him were better suited to the childish imagination.

'Señor Simón, you have been through a testing time. I can see you are upset. I am upset too. The death of a child is a terrible thing. Let us take up this conversation again when we are more in control of our feelings.'

'No, on the contrary, señora, let us complete this conversation now, while our feelings are out of our control. David knew he was dying. He found solace in the belief that after death he would be translated into the heavens among the stars. Why disillusion him? Why tell him his faith was extravagant? Do you not believe in a life to come?'

'I do. I do. But the life to come will be here on earth, not among the dead stars. We will die, all of us, and disintegrate, and become the material for a new generation to rise up from. There will be a life after this one, but I, the one I call *I*, will not be here to live it. Nor will you. Nor will David. Now please let me go.'

CHAPTER 20

THERE IS the matter of the body, of what the hospital calls *los restos físicos*, the physical remains. The orphanage of Las Manos is recorded as David's place of residence and the director of the orphanage as his guardian, therefore it is up to Dr Fabricante to decide how the remains are to be disposed of. Until such time as Dr Fabricante communicates his decision, the remains are in the care of the hospital and will be stored in a refrigerated space to which members of the public will not have access. So he learns from the woman at the desk.

'I am familiar with what you call a refrigerated space,' he tells her. 'It is in fact a room in the basement. I have been there myself, I was let in by one of the orderlies. Señora, I am not just a member of the public. For the past four years my wife and I have taken care of David. We have fed him and clothed him and seen to his welfare. We have loved and cherished him. All we ask is to spend tonight watching over him. Please! It is not a lot to ask. Do you want the poor child to spend the first night of his death alone? No! The thought is unbearable.'

The woman at the desk – he does not know her name – is of the same age as he. They have got on well in the past. He does not envy her her job, coping with distraught parents, holding the official line. He is not proud of himself, making his appeal to her.

'Please,' he says. 'We will be invisible.'

'I will discuss it with my superior,' she says. 'He should not have let you in, Dmitri, if it was Dmitri who did it. He could get into trouble.'

'I don't want anyone to get into trouble. What I am asking for is perfectly reasonable. You have children, I am sure. You would not do it to a child of your own – let the poor thing spend the night alone.'

Behind him in the queue is a young woman with a baby on her hip. He turns to her. 'Would you do it, señora? No, of course you would not.'

The young mother looks away in embarrassment. He is being shameless, he knows it, but this is not an ordinary day.

'I will speak to my superior,' repeats the woman at the desk. He was under the impression that she liked him, but perhaps he was mistaken. There is nothing friendly in her aspect. She wants him to go away: that is all she cares about.

'When will you speak to your superior?'

'When I have a chance. When I have attended to these people.'

He comes back an hour later, taking his place at the end of the queue.

'What is the decision?' he asks, when his turn comes. 'About David.'

'I am sorry, but it cannot be allowed. There are reasons, which

I cannot go into, but they concern the cause of death. Let me simply say, there are rules we have to follow.'

'What do you mean, the cause of death?'

'The cause of death is undecided. Until the cause of death is decided, there are rules we have to follow.'

'And there are no exceptions to these rules, even for a little boy on the worst day of his life?'

'This is a hospital, señor. What has happened happens here every day, and we grieve for it, but your boy is not an exception.'

In the confusion of David's last days, Bolívar has been left to himself in Inés's apartment, neglected and only irregularly fed. When he and Inés return from the hospital that evening, he is gone.

Since the door was not locked, their first surmise is that Bolívar had been howling and a neighbour, irritated by the noise, had let him out. He makes a tour of the neighbourhood but fails to find him. Suspecting that the dog may be trying to find his way back to David, he borrows Inés's car and drives back to the hospital. But no one there has seen him.

First thing in the morning he telephones Las Manos and speaks to Fabricante's secretary. 'If by any chance a large dog appears at the orphanage, will you let me know?' he says.

'I am not a dog-lover,' says the secretary.

'I am not asking you to love the dog, merely to report his presence,' he says. 'Surely you can do that.'

Inés is full of reproaches. 'If you had kept the door locked this would never have happened,' she says. 'This on top of everything.'

'If it is the last thing I do, I will find him and bring him back,' he promises.

I will bring him back. It does not escape him that he failed to bring back the boy.

On the little printing machine at the depot he prints a handbill in five hundred copies: LOST. LARGE DOG, TAWNY COLORATION, WITH LEATHER COLLAR AND MEDALLION READING BOLÍVAR. REWARD FOR HIS RETURN. He distributes the handbill not only across his sector of the city but across the sectors covered by the other bicycle messengers as well; he pastes it on telegraph poles. All day he is busy; all day he keeps at bay the hole that has opened up in the texture of being.

Soon the telephone starts ringing. There have been sightings of a large dog of tawny coloration all over the city; whether the dog in question wears a medallion with the name Bolívar on it no one can say, since the dog has been either too swift to capture or too menacing to approach.

He writes down the name and address of each caller. By the end of the day he has thirty names and no idea of what to do next. If all the callers are telling the truth, it can only follow that Bolívar has manifested himself in widely separate quarters of the city at virtually the same time. The alternative is that some of the calls have been hoaxes, or else that there are several large, tawny dogs on the loose. Whatever the case, he has no better idea of where to find Bolívar, the real Bolívar.

'Bolívar is an intelligent animal,' he tells Inés. 'If he wants to find his way back to us, he will find his way back.'

'What if he is injured?' she replies. 'What if he has been hit by a car? What if he is dead?'

'I will go to the Asistencia first thing tomorrow morning and get a list of veterinarians. I will visit each of them and leave a copy of my advertisement. One way or another, I will get Bolívar back for you.'

'You said the same about David,' says Inés.

'Inés, if I could have taken his place I would have. Without a moment's hesitation.'

'We should have brought him to Novilla, hospital facilities are much better there. But Dr Ribeiro kept making promises, and we kept believing him. I blame myself, I really do.'

'Blame me, Inés, blame me! I was the one who believed in the promises. I was the gullible one, not you.'

He would say more in the same vein, but then hears how much like Dmitri he sounds, and is ashamed of himself and shuts up. *Blame me, punish me!* How contemptible! What he needs is a sharp slap in the face. *Grow up, Simón! Be a man!*

The next day brings a further half-dozen sightings of Bolívar – the real Bolívar or a spectral Bolívar, who knows? – after which there is silence. Inés returns to the routines of Modas Modernas, he resumes his bicycle round. Sometimes, of an evening, Inés will invite him for a meal; but for the most part they spend their time apart, hurt, grieving.

His round of the veterinary clinics brings one success. At Clínica Jull a nurse leads him into the yard where the animals are housed. 'Is that the dog you are after?' she asks, pointing to a cage in which a huge dog of tawny coloration stalks up and down. 'He does not have a name-tag, but he may have had one and lost it.'

The dog is not Bolívar. He is years younger. But he has Bolívar's eyes and Bolívar's air of quiet menace too.

'No, it is not Bolívar,' he says. 'What is his story?'

'A man brought him in last week. Said his name is Pablo. His wife gave birth recently and was afraid Pablo might molest the baby while her back was turned. Dogs get jealous, as I am sure you know. He tried to give him away, but no one in their circle wanted him.'

He stands before Pablo whom no one wants, inspecting him. For a moment the yellow eyes pass over him, and a shiver runs down his spine. Then the eyes slide off and the gaze goes blank again.

'What does the future hold for Pablo?' he asks.

'We do not like to put an animal down if it is healthy. So we will hold him as long as we can. But you cannot keep a handsome fellow like that locked up indefinitely. It is too cruel.' She gives him an interrogatory look. 'What do you think?'

'I don't know what I think. Is death ever better than life, even life locked up in a cage? Maybe we should ask Pablo for his thoughts.'

'I meant: What do you think about taking him, giving him a home?'

What does he think? He thinks Inés will be outraged. *Today you bring home a stray dog, tomorrow you will bring home a stray child.*

'I will see what my wife says,' he says. 'If she is agreeable, I will come back. But I fear she will not agree. She is very attached to our Bolívar. She still hopes he will return. If he ever does return, and finds a stranger sleeping in his bed, he will kill him. As simple as that. Kill or be killed. But let us see. Maybe I am wrong. Goodbye, and thank you. Goodbye, Pablo.'

He pleads Pablo's cause to Inés. 'What do we know about dogs?' he says. 'Human beings die and then wake up as new selves in a new world. Maybe when dogs die they wake up in the same world, this world, again and again. Maybe that is a dog's destiny. Maybe that is what it means to be a dog. But do you not find it strange that fate should lead me to a cage holding a dog who could easily be Bolívar as Bolívar was ten years ago? Won't you at least come and take a look? You will be able to tell at once whether he is Bolívar re-embodied or just another dog.'

Inés is unmoved. 'Bolívar is not dead,' she says. 'We neglected him, we forgot to feed him, he felt abandoned, he left us. He is wandering around somewhere in the city, eating out of bins.'

'If you will not give a home to Pablo, I may be forced to take him myself,' he says. 'I can't just let him be put down. It is too unfair.'

'Do as you wish,' says Inés. 'But then he will be your dog, not mine.'

He returns to the clinic. 'I have decided to take Pablo,' he announces.

'I am afraid you are too late,' says the nurse. 'A couple came in yesterday, soon after you, and adopted him with no hesitation. He was just what they were looking for, they said. They run a poultry farm on the outskirts of the city. They need a dog who will keep predators away.'

'Can you give me their address?'

'I am sorry, I am not allowed to do that.'

'Then could you let this farming couple know that if it does not work out, if for some reason Pablo turns out not to be the dog they are looking for, there is someone else who will offer him a home?'

'I will do that.'

There is something crazy – he can see it all too clearly – in his quest for Bolívar. No wonder Inés is so abrupt with him. The body of their son has not been laid to rest – in fact no one seems prepared to tell them straight out what has become of the body – yet here he is, scouring the city for a runaway dog. What is wrong with him?

He buys a pot of paint, visits all the walls and lamp posts he can remember where he pasted his LOST notices, and blacks them out. *Give up*, he tells himself. *The dog is gone.*

He cannot claim to have loved Bolívar. He was not even fond of him. But then, love was never an appropriate feeling to have for Bolívar. Bolívar demanded something quite different: to be left alone in his being. He, Simón, respected that demand. In return the dog left him alone in his being, and perhaps left Inés alone too.

With David it was a different story. In a sense Bolívar was a normal dog, overindulged perhaps, lazy perhaps, in his late years somewhat gluttonous perhaps, a dog who did a lot of sleeping, who in some accountings could be said to have slept his life away. But in another sense Bolívar never slept, not when David was around, or, if he slept, slept with one eye open, one ear cocked, watching over him, keeping him from harm. If Bolívar had a lord and master, David was he.

Until the end. Until the great harm came from which he could not save his master. Is that perhaps the deeper reason why Bolívar is gone: he has gone to find his master, wherever he may be, find him and bring him back?

Dogs do not understand death, do not understand how a being can cease to be. But perhaps the reason (the deeper reason) why they do not understand death is that they do not understand understanding. I Bolívar breathe my last in a gutter in the rain-lashed city and at the same moment I Pablo find myself in a wire cage in a stranger's backyard. What is there that demands to be understood in that?

He, Simón, is learning. First he went to school with a child, now he is going to school with a dog. A life of learning. He ought to be thankful.

He visits the Asistencia again. This time he asks for a list of poultry farms. The Asistencia has no such list. *Go to the market*, the clerk advises him: *ask around*. He goes to the market and asks around. One thing leads to another; soon he is standing at the door of a galvanized iron shed in the valley above the city, calling out, 'Hello! Is anyone here?'

A young woman emerges, wearing rubber boots, smelling of ammonia.

'Good day, I am sorry to trouble you,' he says, 'but have you recently taken in a dog from Dr Jull the veterinarian?'

The young woman whistles cheerily and a dog comes bounding up. It is Pablo.

'I saw this dog while he was being held in Dr Jull's backyard and wanted very much to take him, but by the time I had consulted my wife he was gone. I do not know what you paid, but I am prepared to offer you a hundred reales.'

The young woman shakes her head. 'Pablo is just what we need here. He is not for sale.'

He thinks of telling her about Bolívar – about Bolívar's place in his life, in Inés's life, in the life of the boy, about the gap that has been left by the double departure of the dog and the boy, about his vision of Bolívar lying dead in a gutter in the back streets of the city and his second vision of Bolívar re-embodied in Pablo – but then decides not to, it is too complicated. 'Let me leave my telephone number,' he says. 'My offer stands. A hundred reales, two hundred, whatever it takes. Goodbye, Pablo.' He stretches out a hand to stroke the dog's head. The dog flattens his ears and growls low in his throat. 'Goodbye, señora.'

CHAPTER 21

HE AND Inés sit in silence over the remains of a meal.

'Is this how we are going to spend the rest of our days, you and I?' he says at last. 'Growing old in a city where neither of us feels at home, mourning our loss?'

Inés does not reply.

'Inés, can I tell you something David said to me shortly before the end? He said he thought that after he was gone you and I would have a child together. I did not know how to reply. In the end I said you and I did not have that kind of relationship. But have you thought of adopting a child – one of the children from the orphanage, for instance? Or several? Have you thought of the two of us starting again from the beginning and raising a proper family?'

Inés gives him a cold, hostile look. Why? Is his proposal contemptible?

He and Inés have been together for over four years, long enough to have seen the worst of each other, and the best. Neither is, to the other, an unknown quantity.

'Answer me, Inés. Why not start all over, before it is too late?'

'Too late for what?'

'Before we are too old – too old to bring up children.'

'No,' says Inés. 'I do not want a child from the orphanage in my home, sleeping in my child's bed. It is an insult. I am astonished at you.'

There are nights when he wakes up with what he can swear is the boy's voice ringing in his ears: *Simón, I can't sleep, come and tell me a story!* or *Simón, I am having a bad dream!* or *Simón, I am lost, come and save me!* He presumes the voice comes to Inés too, unsettling her sleep, but he does not ask.

He avoids the football games in the park behind the apartment block. But sometimes, in the figure of a child dashing across the road or scampering up the stairway, he glimpses the image of David and feels a gust of the bitterest resentment that his child alone should be taken away while the ninety-nine others are left unscathed to play and be happy. It seems monstrous that the darkness should have swallowed him up, that there should be no outcry, no clamour, no tearing of hair or gnashing of teeth, that the world should continue to spin on its axis as if nothing had happened.

He calls at the Academy to pick up David's belongings, and without knowing how or why finds himself in Arroyo's chambers laying bare his heart. 'I am ashamed to confess to it, Juan Sebastián, but I look at David's young friends and find myself wishing they had died in his place – one of them, all of them, it makes no difference. An evil spirit, a spirit of pure malignancy, seems to have taken possession of me and I cannot shake it off.'

'Do not be too harsh with yourself, Simón,' says Arroyo. 'The turmoil you feel will pass, given time. A door opens, a child enters; the same door closes, the child is gone, all is as it was before. Nothing in the world has changed. Yet it is not so, not quite. Even if we cannot see it, hear it, feel it, the earth has shifted.' Arroyo pauses, regards him intently. 'Something has occurred, Simón, something that is not nothing. When you feel the bitterness rising in you, remember that.'

There is a cloud over his brain, or else the spirit of darkness is at work, but at this moment he cannot see it, certainly cannot grasp it, Arroyo's *something that is not nothing*. What mark has David left behind? None. None at all. Not so much as the beat of a butterfly's wing.

Arroyo speaks. 'If I may change the subject, colleagues of mine have suggested that we gather together formally, staff and students, to pay our respects to your son. Will you and Inés join us?'

Arroyo is as good as his word. The very next morning activities at the Academy are suspended as students assemble to honour their lost classmate. He and Inés are the only outsiders present.

Arroyo addresses the gathering. 'David arrived among us years ago as a student of dance, but soon revealed himself to be not a student but a teacher, a teacher to all of us. I do not need to remind you how when he danced for us we would stand still in wonder.

'The privilege fell to me to be among his students. In our sessions together I would play the part of musician and he the part of dancer, but truly, when he began to dance, dance became music and music became dance. From him the dance flowed into my

151

hands and fingers, and into my spirit too. I was the instrument on which he played. He exalted me, as I know from your testimonies he exalted you too, and everyone whose life he touched.

'The music I will play for you today is music I learned from him. When the music has ended we will observe a minute of silent reflection. Then we will disperse, bearing the memory of his music within us.'

Arroyo sits down at the organ and begins to play. At once he, Simón, recognizes the measure. It is the measure of Seven, elaborated with an unfamiliar sweetness and grace. He feels for Inés's hand, grips it, closes his eyes, gives himself over to the music.

From the stairway comes a sudden clatter, and a surge of young bodies bursts into the studio. At their head is Maria Prudencia from the orphanage bearing a placard pinned to a stick. LOS DESINVITADOS, it reads: the uninvited. Behind her, side by side, come Dr Fabricante and señora Devito, followed by a host of orphans, as many as a hundred. In their midst, borne on the shoulders of four of the older boys, is a simple coffin, painted white, which, in a planned manoeuvre, they convey to the stage and set down.

Dr Fabricante gives a nod, and the four coffin-bearers are joined on the stage by señora Devito. Through all this Arroyo makes no move to intervene: he seems bemused.

Señora Devito addresses the gathering. 'Friends!' she calls out. 'This is a sad occasion for all of you. You have lost one of your number; there is a gap in your midst. But I bring you a message, and the message is a joyous one. The coffin you see before you, which has been borne through the streets of the city all the way from Las Manos on the shoulders of these young comrades of

David, is a symbol of his death but also of his life. Maria! Esteban!'

Maria and the tall pimply youth who is her companion step up and, without a word, upend the coffin and slide the lid aside. The coffin is empty.

Esteban speaks. His voice is unsteady, his face is flushed, he is clearly uncomfortable. 'We, the orphans of Las Manos, having been present at the bedside of David during his last travails, decided …' He casts a desperate look at Maria, who whispers in his ear. 'Decided that we would celebrate his passing by passing on his message.'

Now it is Maria's turn. She speaks with unexpected composure. 'We call this the coffin of David, and as you can see it is empty. What does that say to us? It says to us that he is not gone, that he is still with us. Why is the coffin white? Because this may feel like a sad day but it is not really a sad day. That is all. That is what we wanted to say.'

Dr Fabricante gives another nod. The orphans replace the lid on the coffin and hoist it upon their shoulders. 'Thank you, all of you,' señora Devito calls out above the noise. She wears a smile that he can only call rapturous. 'Thank you for permitting the children of Las Manos, too often passed over and forgotten, to take part in your memorial.' And, as abruptly as they had arrived, the orphans file out of the studio and down the stairs, bearing the coffin with them.

The next morning, as he and Inés are having breakfast, Alyosha comes knocking at the door. 'Señor Arroyo asks me to beg your pardon for the chaos yesterday. We were taken completely by surprise. Also, you forgot these.' He holds out David's dancing slippers.

Without a word Inés takes the slippers and leaves the room.

'Inés is upset,' he says. 'It has not been easy for her. I am sure you understand. Shall we go outdoors, you and I? We could take a walk in the park.'

It is a pleasant day, cool, wind-still. The sound of their footsteps is muffled by a thick bed of fallen leaves.

'Did David ever show you his coin trick?' says Alyosha, out of the blue.

'His coin trick?'

'The trick where he flips a coin and it comes up heads every time. Ten times, twenty times, thirty times.'

'He must have had a double-headed coin.'

'He could do it with any coin you gave him.'

'No, he never showed me that particular trick. But until I put a stop to it he used to play at dice with Dmitri, and Dmitri said that David could throw a double six whenever he wanted to. What other tricks did he have?'

'The trick with the coin was the only one I got to see. I was never able to work out how he did it. Something to wonder about.'

'I suppose if one has very fine muscular control one can flip a coin or throw dice in exactly the same way each time. That must be the explanation.'

'He did the trick only to amuse us,' says Alyosha, 'but he did say once that if he wanted to he could use it to bring the pillars crashing down.'

'What on earth did he mean: bring the pillars crashing down?'

'No idea. You know how David was. He would never tell you his meaning directly. Always left it to you to puzzle things out.'

'Did he do his coin trick for Juan Sebastián?'

'No, just for the children in his class. I told Juan Sebastián about it, but he was not interested. He said that nothing David did surprised him.'

'Alyosha, did David ever mention a message he was carrying?'

'A message? No.'

'David divided people up according to whether or not they were fit to hear his message. I fell among the no-hopers – too plodding, too earthbound. I thought he might have elevated you to the other camp, the camp of the elect. I thought he might have revealed his message to you. He was fond of you. You were fond of him too, I could see that.'

'I was not just fond of him, Simón, I loved him. We all did. I would have laid down my life for him. Truly. But no – he gave me no message.'

'On the last night I spent with him he spoke on and on about his message – spoke about it without actually saying what it was. Now Dmitri claims that the message was revealed to him, in full. As you know, ever since the days of Ana Magdalena, Dmitri has insisted there is or was a special bond between David and himself, a secret affinity. I never believed him – he is such a liar. But now, as I say, he is putting out a story that David left a message behind and he alone is its bearer.

'The children at the orphanage have been particularly receptive to his story. That must have been why they invaded the memorial yesterday. David's message was destined for them, says Dmitri, and for the orphans of the world in general, but he died too early to deliver it in person, so only he, Dmitri, got to hear the whole of it. He is using his friend from the hospital to spread the story. You saw her yesterday: the petite woman with the blonde hair. She backs up everything he says.'

'And what is the message, according to Dmitri?'

'He will not say. I am not surprised. That is how he operates – keeping his opponents guessing. In my opinion the whole thing is *una estafa*, a confidence trick. If he does have a message, it is one he himself has made up.'

'I thought Dmitri was sentenced to be locked up for life. How does he come to be free again?'

'Goodness knows. He claims to have seen the error of his ways and repented. He claims to be a new man, reformed. He is plausible. People want to believe him, or at least to give him the benefit of the doubt.'

'Well, you should hear what Juan Sebastián has to say about him.'

That evening he speaks to Inés. 'Inés, did David ever show you a trick he could do, tossing a coin and making it come up heads every time?'

'No.'

'Alyosha says he used to do the trick for his schoolmates. And did he ever tell you about a message he was going to leave behind?'

Inés turns to face him. 'Does everything have to be brought out into the open, Simón? Can I not have a little space that is my own?'

'I am sorry, I had no idea you felt that way.'

'You have no idea how I feel about anything. Have you ever considered how I felt when I was shunted aside by those people at the hospital – *We are looking for the real mother, you are not the real mother, go away* – as if David were some foundling, some *orphan*? You may find insults like that easy to swallow, but I do not. As far as I am concerned, David was taken from me when he most needed me, and I will never forgive the people who took him, never, including that Dr Fabricante.'

It is clear he has touched a raw nerve. He tries to take her hand, but she pushes him off angrily. 'Go away. Leave me alone. You are just making things worse.'

Relations with Inés have never been easy. Though they have been in Estrella for four years, she remains restless, unsettled, unhappy. More often than not, he is the one she chooses to blame for her unhappiness: he was the one who stole her away from Novilla and the pleasing life she led there in the company of her brothers. Yet the fact is, David could not have had a more devoted mother. He, Simón, has been devoted too, in his way. But he could always foresee the day when the boy would shrug him off for good (*You can't tell me what to do, you are not my father*). In the case of Inés the bond seemed altogether stronger and deeper, altogether less easy to escape from.

Inés begrudged the loss of freedom that was the price of motherhood, yet she was unquestioningly devoted to her son. If this was a contradiction, she seemed to have no difficulty in living with it.

In an ideal world he and Inés, as parents of David, would

have loved each other as much as they loved their son. In the less than ideal world in which they found themselves, the anger that simmered beneath the surface in Inés found an outlet in bouts of coldness or irritability directed at him, to which he responded by absenting himself. With the child gone, how much longer can they hope to stay together?

As the days go by, Inés reminisces more and more openly about the old days at La Residencia. She misses the tennis, she says, she misses the swimming, she misses her brothers, particularly the younger, Diego, whose girlfriend is expecting a second child.

'If that is how you feel, maybe you should go back,' he tells her. 'What is there to keep you in Estrella, after all, besides the shop? You are still young. You have your life before you.'

Inés smiles mysteriously, seems on the point of saying something, then does not.

'Have you thought what we should do with David's clothes?' he says during one of their silent evenings together.

'Are you proposing that I give them to that orphanage? Absolutely not. I would rather burn them.'

'That is not what I am suggesting. If we gave them to the orphanage they would in all likelihood put them in a showcase as relics. No, I was thinking of giving the clothes to a charity.'

'Do as you wish, just do not talk to me about it.'

She does not want to discuss the future of the boy's clothes, but he cannot help noticing that Bolívar's feeding dish has disappeared from the kitchen, together with his cushion.

While Inés is out he packs David's clothes into two suitcases, from the frilled shirt and the shoes with straps that Inés bought when she adopted him to the white shirt with the number 9 on the back that he wore on the hopeful day when he went to play football at Las Manos.

He buries his nose in the number 9 shirt. Does he imagine it, or does the fabric still carry the faint cinnamon odour of the boy's skin?

He knocks on the door of the caretaker's apartment. It is opened by the caretaker's wife. 'Good day,' he says. 'We haven't met. I am Simón, I am in A-13, across the yard. My son used to play football with your son. My son David. Please do not take it amiss, but I know you have small children, and my wife and I wonder whether you would not like David's clothes. Otherwise they will just go to waste.' He opens the first of the suitcases. 'As you can see, they are in good condition. David was careful with his clothes.'

The woman seems flustered. 'I am so sorry,' she says. 'I mean, I am so sorry for your loss.'

He closes the suitcase. 'My apologies,' he says. 'I should not have asked. It was stupid of me.'

'There is a charity shop on Calle Rosa, next door to the post office. I am sure they will be glad to take them.'

There are nights when Inés does not come home until past midnight. He waits up, listening for her car, for the sound of her footsteps as she climbs the stairs.

On one of these late evenings the footsteps pause at his door.

She knocks. She is distraught, he sees at once, has perhaps had too much to drink.

'I can't take it any more, Simón,' she says, and begins to cry.

He folds her in his arms. Her handbag falls to the floor. She wriggles free and recovers it. 'I don't know what to do,' she says. 'I can't go on like this.'

'Sit down, Inés,' he says. 'I will make some tea.'

She throws herself on the sofa. A moment later she is up again. 'Don't make tea, I am leaving,' she says.

He catches her at the door, leads her back to the sofa, sits down beside her. 'Inés, Inés,' he says, 'you have suffered a terrible loss, we have both suffered a terrible loss, you are not yourself, how could it be otherwise? We are mutilated beings. I have no words that can take away your pain, but if you need to cry, cry on my shoulder.' Then he holds her while she sobs and sobs.

This is the first of three nights they spend together, sleeping in his bed. There is no question of sex; but on the third night, given courage by the dark, Inés begins, at first hesitantly, then more and more freely, to tell her story, a story that goes back to the day when the idyll of La Residencia came to its abrupt end with the arrival, uninvited, unwelcome, of a strange man with a boy-child clutching his hand.

'He looked so lonely, so helpless in those clothes you made him wear that did not fit – my heart went out to him. Never until that day had I thought of myself as a mother. What other women spoke about – the craving, the yearning, whatever they called it – was simply not in me. But there was such entreaty in those big eyes of his – I could not resist. If I had been able to see into the future, if I had known how much pain I was letting myself in for, I would have refused. But at that moment there was nothing I could say but: *You have chosen me, little one. I am yours, take me.*'

That is not how he, Simón, remembers the day. As he remembers, it had required a great deal of pleading and persuasion to bring Inés around. *David did not exactly choose you, Inés,* he would like to say (but does not because experience has taught him it is unwise to contradict her) – *no, he recognized you. He recognized you as his mother, he recognized his mother in you. And in return* (he would like to go on, but does not) *he wanted you – he wanted both of us – to recognize him. That was what he demanded again and again: to be recognized. Though* (he would like to add in conclusion) *how an ordinary person can be expected to recognize someone he has never seen before is beyond me.*

'It was (Inés presses on with her monologue) as if, all at once, my future grew clear to me. Until then, living in La Residencia, I had always felt a bit extraneous, a bit isolated, as if I were floating. Suddenly I was brought down to earth. There was work to do. I had someone to take care of. I had a purpose. And now ...' She breaks off; in the dark he can hear her fighting back tears. 'And now, what is left?'

'We have been lucky, Inés,' he says, trying to console her. 'We could have lived our ordinary lives, you in your sphere, I in mine, and no doubt we would each have found contentment of a kind. But what would it have added up to, in the end, that ordinary contentment? Instead we had the privilege of being visited by a comet. I remember something Juan Sebastián said to me just recently: David arrived, the world changed, David departed, and the world has gone back to being as it was before. That is what you and I cannot bear: the thought that he has been erased, that nothing is left behind, that he may as well not have existed. Yet it is not true. *It is not true!* The world may be as it was before, but it is also different. We must hold tight to that difference, you and I, even if for the present we cannot see it.'

'It was like finding myself in a fairy story, those first months,' Inés continues. Her voice is low, dreamy; he doubts she has heard a word of what he has just said. '*Una luna de miel*, that was how it was for me, if one is allowed to have a honeymoon with a child. Never had I felt so complete, so satisfied. He was my *caballerito*, my little man. For hours on end I used to stand over him while he slept, drinking in the sight of him, aching with love. You don't understand it, do you – a mother's love? How could you?'

'No indeed – how could I? But it was clear to me from the first how much you loved him. You are not a demonstrative person, but anyone could see it, even a stranger.'

'Those were the best days of my life. Later, when he started going to school, things became more difficult. He began to pull away from me, to resist. But I don't want to go into that.'

She does not need to. He remembers those days all too well, remembers the taunt: *You can't tell me what to do, you are not my real mother!*

Across the yawning space between his side of the bed and hers, through the curtain of darkness, he speaks: 'He loved you, Inés, whatever he may have said in his impulsive way. He was your child, yours and no one else's.'

'He was not my child, Simón. You know that as well as I do.

Even less was he yours. He was a wild creature, a creature out of the forest. He did not belong to anyone. Certainly not to us.'

A wild creature: her words give him a jolt. He would not have thought her capable of such insight. Inés, full of surprises.

That marks the close of Inés's long confession. Without touching, maintaining a wary distance, they consign themselves to sleep, first she, then he. When he wakes she is gone, and does not return.

Days later he finds a slip of paper under his door. The handwriting is hers. 'A message to call Alyosha at the Academy. Please do not involve me in any arrangements.'

CHAPTER 22

'I HAVE a proposal to put before you,' says Alyosha. 'It comes from the boys, from David's friends, with the blessing of Juan Sebastián. It is that we stage a fresh event, *un espectáculo* in memory of David. Something fitting but not too sombre, not too sad. Restricted to children from the Academy and their parents. So that we can celebrate him properly, without interference from outsiders. Will you give your permission?'

The plan was dreamed up, it emerges, by Juan Sebastián's sons Joaquín and Damián.

At first they had simply proposed to perform dances in which David would be evoked; now they want the dances to be supplemented with comic sketches, episodes from David's life. 'They would like it to be a children's affair, something light-hearted,' says Alyosha. 'They want us to remember David as he was in real life, not to make us cry. We have cried enough, they say.'

'David as he was in real life,' he says. 'How much do the children at the Academy know about David's real life?'

'Enough,' says Alyosha. 'It is an end-of-term entertainment, not a history project.'

'If Juan Sebastián is serious about his *espectáculo*, I have an alternative proposal to make. He and I could buy a donkey and tour the land giving performances. He could play the violin, I could dance. We could call ourselves the Gypsy Brothers and call our show "The Deeds of David".'

Alyosha is dubious. 'I don't think Juan Sebastián would like the idea. I don't think he has time to go touring.'

'Just a joke, Alyosha. Don't bother to repeat it to Juan Sebastián. He won't find it funny. So he wants to hold a second event. Let me put the idea to Inés and see what she says.'

Once upon a time he had had high hopes for Alyosha. But the handsome young teacher has been a bit of a disappointment: too earthbound in his thinking, too literally minded. He claims to be an admirer of David, but how much of the real, the mercurial David could have been visible to him?

At first Inés refuses permission. From the beginning she has had reservations about the Academy – about the education it offers (frivolous, insubstantial), about Arroyo himself (remote, arrogant), about the scandal – not for a moment forgotten – of señora Arroyo's liaison with the school caretaker. He does his best to change her mind. 'The show comes as an offering from the children themselves,' he urges. 'You cannot punish them for the shortcomings of the Academy. They loved David. They want to do something in memory of him.' Grudgingly Inés comes around.

The event, held in the afternoon and at short notice, brings in a surprisingly large number of parents. Arroyo does not address the gathering himself, or appear onstage. Instead the show is introduced by Joaquín, his elder son, who has turned into a serious, even scholarly fourteen-year-old. Joaquín speaks to the audience with no sign of nervousness. 'We all know David, so I don't need to explain him,' he says. 'The first half of our programme is called The Acts and Sayings of David. The second half will be dance and music. That is all. We hope you will enjoy it.'

Two boys march out onto the stage. One has a chaplet on his head with a big letter D inked on it. The other wears an academic gown and mortarboard; a cushion is tied around his waist under the gown to give him a bulging belly.

'Boy, what is two and two?' demands the teacher figure in a booming voice.

'Two what and two what?' replies the David figure.

'What a stupid boy he is!' says the teacher in a loud, exasperated aside. 'Two apples and two apples, boy. Or two oranges and two oranges. Two units and two units. Two and two.'

'What is a unit?' asks David.

'A unit is anything, it can be an apple, it can be an orange, it can be anything in the universe. Do not test my patience, boy! Two and two!'

'Can it be snot?' says David.

There is an eruption of laughter from the audience. The boy playing the teacher starts giggling too. The cushion slips out and falls with a plop on the stage. More laughter. The two boys take a bow and exit.

Two new actors take the stage. The boy who had played David comes running back and hands over the chaplet, which one of the newcomers dons.

'What is that behind your back?' says the David figure.

The other reveals what he has been hiding: a bowl full of toffees.

'I will wager with you,' says David. 'I will toss a coin and if it comes up heads you must give me a toffee and if it comes up tails I will give you everything.'

'Everything?' says the second boy. 'What do you mean by everything?'

'Everything in the universe,' says David. 'Are you ready?'

He tosses his coin. 'Heads,' he announces. The second boy hands over a toffee. 'Again?' says the David boy. The second boy nods. He tosses his coin. 'Heads,' he announces. He holds out a hand for a toffee.

'That is not fair,' says the second boy. 'It is a trick coin.'

'It is not a trick coin,' says David. 'Give me another coin.'

With elaborate show the second boy fishes a coin from his pocket. David tosses the new coin. 'Heads,' he announces, and holds out his hand.

The routine accelerates: the toss, the announcement ('Heads'), the held-out hand, the handover of the toffee. Soon the bowl is empty. 'What are you going to wager now?' says David. 'I'll wager my shirt,' says the second boy. He loses his shirt, then a shoe, then the other shoe. At last he stands clad only in his underpants. David tosses the coin, but this time says no word, neither 'Heads' nor 'Tails', but gives a meaningful smile. The second boy breaks down in tears: 'Boo-hoo-hoo!' The two take a bow, to a storm of applause.

An iron bedstead is dragged onto the stage, with a sheet

draped over it. The younger Arroyo boy, wearing mustachios and a pointed beard and a nightshirt down to his ankles, lies on the bed, crosses his arms on his chest, closes his eyes.

Alyosha enters, dressed in a dark overcoat. 'So, Don Quixote,' says Alyosha, 'here you lie on your deathbed. The time has come for you to make your peace with the world. No more dragons to kill, no more damsels to rescue. Will you acknowledge that it was all *una tontería*, a load of rubbish, the life you led as a knight errant?'

Don Quixote does not stir.

'The giant whom you charged so valiantly, you and Rocinante – in truth it was no giant but a mere windmill. None of it was real, this life of adventure that you led. It was all a show put on to entertain us. You knew that, did you not? You were an actor, playing a part, and we were your audience. But now the show is coming to an end. Time to hang up your sword. Time to confess. Speak, Don Quixote!'

Damián Arroyo, with his beard somewhat askew, sits up in bed with an elaborate show of creakiness. In a quavering voice he speaks: 'Bring me Rocinante!'

A horse emerges from the wings: two children crouching beneath a red carpet, only their legs visible, bearing a papier-mâché horse's head before them.

'Bring me my sword!' commands Damián.

A child clad in black comes onstage bearing a painted wooden sword, which he hands over.

Descending from his bed, Damián faces the audience, raises his sword on high. 'Forth, Rocinante!' he cries out. 'While there are damsels to save, we shall not cease!' He tries to clamber onto the back of Rocinante. The boys under the carpet stagger and fall. The horse-head clatters to the floor. Damián waves the sword above his head. His beard falls off but the mustachios remain in place. 'Forth, Rocinante!' he cries again. There is a great cheer. Alyosha embraces him, lifts him bodily, shows him off to the audience.

He, Simón, turns to Inés. Tears pour down her cheeks but she is smiling. He clasps her hand. 'Our boy!' he whispers in her ear.

Two helpers push a capacious cardboard box onto the stage, one side of it cut away. Wearing a long black robe, a green wig and stark white face-paint, a boy actor emerges from the wings, steps into the box, and stands there in silence, hanging his head.

There is a rattle of drumbeats and Joaquín, wearing the chaplet with the letter D, bearing a heavy staff, looking regal, marches onstage. He seats himself on a chair facing the box.

He speaks. 'Your name is El Lobo, the wolf.'

'Yes, my lord,' replies the figure in black, still hanging his head.

'Your name is El Lobo and you are charged with devouring an innocent puppy who did you no harm, who wanted only to play. How do you plead?'

'Guilty, my lord. I ask for your forgiveness. It is my nature to eat little animals, lambs and puppies and kittens and so forth. The more innocent they are, the more appetizing I find them. I cannot help myself.'

'If it is your nature to eat puppies then it is my nature to pronounce judgement. Are you ready to be judged, El Lobo?'

'I am, my lord. Judge me harshly. Let me be beaten with whips. Let me suffer for my bad nature. I beg only that after I have suffered my punishment you will forgive me.'

'No, El Lobo, until you change your nature you will not be forgiven. Now I will pronounce sentence. You are sentenced to return the puppy you devoured to life.'

'Boo-hoo!' says the boy in black, ostentatiously wiping away tears. 'Just as it is not in my power to change my nature, so it is not in my power to return the puppy to life, much as I would like to. The puppy in question has been dismembered and chewed up and swallowed down and digested. He is no more. There is no puppy. What used to be a puppy has become part of me. What you demand is impossible to perform.'

'You are wrong, El Lobo! To the king of the world all things are possible!' He rises, bangs his staff three times. 'I decree that the puppy shall be returned to life!'

Alarmed, cowed, the boy in black crouches down in his box so that only his lurid green hair is visible. There are loud sounds of vomiting, one spasm after another. From the back of the box a little figure pops out, whom he, Simón, recognizes at once as El Perrito from the apartments. Bursting with glee, El Perrito skips around the stage while the audience laughs and cheers.

Holding hands, the three actors take a bow: El Perrito, the boy with the green wig, and, wearing the letter D, Joaquín.

The theatrics are over. The clutter is cleared from the stage. On the organ Arroyo improvises a gentle melody. The audience settles. The two Arroyo boys emerge in their tights and dancing slippers. The younger commences the familiar dance of Three. Then as the music grows more complex the older boy launches himself into the dance of Five. Obeying two different rhythms, they circle each other.

Above the rhythms of Three and Five there emerges on the organ a rhythm that crosses both. At first he, Simón, cannot identify it. Too much is going on in this music, he thinks to himself, too much for the mind to follow. In Inés, in the people around him, he can sense the same confusion.

The two Arroyo boys continue their elegant sweeps, circling each other but extending their radius until the centre of the stage is left bare. The music begins to simplify too. First the rhythm of Five drops out, then the rhythm of Three. Only Seven is left. So it continues for a while. The audience relaxes. The music grows softer, ceases. The two boys are still, their heads bowed. The lights dim, the stage is dark, the dance is over.

The show comes to an end with a performance by Arroyo himself on the violin. It is not a success. The audience is restive, there is still too much excitement in the air, and the music itself, quiet, ruminative, is not easy to follow: like a restless bird, it seems unable to make up its mind where to settle. There is applause when it comes to an end, but in the applause he, Simón, detects more than a little relief.

Parents come up to Inés and him. 'Such a beautiful show!... So touching!... Such a loss!... We feel with you ... What a sweet child he was!... And the Arroyo boys were so good, so talented!...'

Moved by the kind words, the kind gestures, he feels an urge to ascend the stage and pour out his heart. *Dear parents, dear children, dear señor Arroyo*, he wants to say, *this day has been unforgettable. David's mother and I carry away imperishable memories of the loving kindness with which our son was nurtured within these walls. Long may the Academy prosper!* But he bethinks himself, holds his tongue, waits for the audience to disperse.

Arroyo stands at the door shaking hands, gravely accepting congratulations. He and Inés are last in the line.

'Thank you, Juan Sebastián,' says Inés, giving him her hand. 'You have made us very proud.' There is a warmth in her voice that surprises him, Simón. 'Thank you most of all for the music.'

'You approved of the music?' says Juan Sebastián.

'Yes. I feared there would be trumpets. I would not have liked trumpets.'

'In my stumbling way, señora, I try to reveal what has been hidden. In such music there is no place for trumpets or drums.'

Arroyo's words puzzle him, but Inés seems to understand. 'Goodnight, Juan Sebastián,' she says.

In an old-fashioned, courtly way, Arroyo bows and kisses her hand.

'What did Juan Sebastián mean?' he asks Inés in the car. 'What is the hidden that he is trying to reveal?'

But Inés only smiles and shakes her head.

CHAPTER 23

THERE IS the unsettled matter of the earthly remains.

He calls the orphanage, speaks to Fabricante's secretary. 'David's mother and I would like to pay a visit to the place where David is interred,' he says. 'Can you tell us where to go?'

'Will it be just the two of you?'

'Just the two of us.'

'Meet me outside the office and I will conduct you,' she says. 'Come in the morning while the children are in class.'

He and Inés – Inés wearing severe black – duly arrive the next morning. The secretary leads them along a winding path through the rose garden to where three modest bronze plaques are set in the brick wall of the assembly hall. 'David's is the one on the right,' she says. 'The most recent.'

He steps closer and reads the plaque. *David*, it says. *Recordado con afecto.* He reads the other two. *Tomás. Recordado con afecto. Emiliano. Recordado con afecto.*

'Is that all?' he says. 'Who are Tomás and Emiliano?'

'Brothers who died in an accident some years ago. The ashes

are in a little compartment behind each plaque.'

'And *Recordado con afecto*, remembered with affection? Is that all your orphanage can manage? No mention of love? Of undying memory? No looking forward to reunion on the farther shore?' He turns to Inés in her stiff black dress and unappealing black hat. 'What do you think? Is affection enough for our child?'

Inés shakes her head.

'David's mother and I are at one,' he says. 'We do not believe *afecto* is enough. It may have been enough for Tomás and Emiliano, I don't know one way or the other, but for David it is not enough, far from enough. Either you change it or I will have it changed.'

'We are a public institution,' says the secretary. 'An institution for the living, not the dead.'

'And the flowers?' He points to a posy of wildflowers against the wall beneath the three plaques. 'Are the flowers institutional too?'

'I have no idea who left the flowers,' says the secretary. 'Probably one of the children.'

'At least there is someone here who has a heart,' he says.

To Alyosha he recounts their visit to the orphanage. 'We were not expecting a grand monument. But it was Dr Fabricante and his people who laid claim to the body. They hovered overhead like vultures and descended on him while we were still numb with grief. Yet once they had him in their claws, they could not have treated him more indifferently, with less *afecto*.'

'You must make allowance for the politics of the situation,' says Alyosha. 'We at the Academy may have our problems, but it is far worse for Dr Fabricante with all those enthusiasts he has to control. You must have heard what they have been up to in the city.'

'No. What have they been up to in the city?'

'Bands of them have been racing from shop to shop, overturning displays, haranguing shopkeepers for charging too much. *The just price!* That is their cry. In one of the pet shops they broke open the cages and set the animals loose – dogs, cats, rabbits, snakes, tortoises. Set the birds loose too. Left only the goldfish. The police had to be called in. All in the cause of the just price, all in the name of David. Some of them claim they have had mystic visions, visions in which David appeared to them and told them his bidding. He has left a huge mark behind. None of which surprises me. You know how David was.'

'I have had no word of this. There is nothing about it in the newspaper. Why do you say David left a mark behind?'

'Look at him through their eyes, Simón, through the eyes of children who have lived in an institution all their lives, following an institutional regime, with hardly any access to the wider world. Suddenly in their midst arrives a child with strange ideas and fantastic stories, a child who has never been schooled, never been tamed, who is scared of no one, certainly not his teachers, who is as beautiful as a girl yet has a flair for football – who arrives in their midst like an apparition, then before they can get used to him falls prey to a mysterious illness and is whisked away, never to set foot in the orphanage again. No wonder they swallow Dmitri's story that he was killed by the men in white coats. No wonder they have turned him into a martyr and a legend.'

'Killed by the doctors? The doctors at the hospital? Is that Dmitri's story? Why would the doctors have wanted to kill David?

They aren't bad people. They are simply incompetent.'

'Not according to Dmitri. According to Dmitri they made up a story about a train that was due to arrive at any minute bringing new blood to save him, then used that story as a cover for sucking the blood out of his body until he wasted away and died.'

'I am dumbfounded. Dmitri is now accusing the doctors of being vampires?'

'No, no, nothing so old-fashioned! The story he puts out is that they drew David's blood into phials which they have stored away in some secret place to use in their nefarious researches.'

'And despite being a psychiatric inmate Dmitri manages to propagate this fantastic nonsense across the city?'

'I don't know how the story is spread, but the children from the orphanage certainly got it from him, and from the orphanage it has fanned out as if with a life of its own. I come back to *con afecto* and the plaque you saw on the wall. You have to appreciate Dr Fabricante's position. If he goes too far in encouraging the enthusiasts, he runs the risk of having his orphanage turned into a shrine and a breeding ground for all kinds of superstition.'

'When you look at what has developed, Alyosha, don't you regret that the Academy failed to lay claim to David, leaving it to Las Manos to take him over? Surely David was more a product of your Academy than he ever was of Las Manos.'

'Yes and no. It is a pity, I agree, that Las Manos has taken ownership of him. But neither Juan Sebastián nor I nor any of the other teachers saw David as a product of the Academy. That would have been laughable. David taught us far more than we taught him. We were his students, all of us, myself included. Do you remember what Juan Sebastián said at the memorial, before we were interrupted, when he described the effect David had on him? He spoke far better than I ever could. It all came down to dance, he said. Somehow or other David translated anything and everything into dance. Dance became the master key or master language, except that it was not a language in the normal sense, with a grammar and a vocabulary and so forth that you could learn out of a book. You could learn only by following. When David danced he was somewhere else, and if you were able to follow him you would be transported to that place too – not always, but now and again, definitely. But I don't need to tell you, you know all this. If I sound incoherent, I am sorry. You should speak to Juan Sebastián, as I said.'

'You are not incoherent at all, my dear Alyosha. On the contrary, you are most eloquent. After the concert last week Juan Sebastián said something that puzzled me. He said that in his music he tried to reveal the hidden. What do you think he meant?'

'You mean in the music he played that day? I have no idea. Ask him. Perhaps he meant that David was one of those people we think are going to have a huge impact on the world but then don't because their lives are cut short. Their lives are cut short so they remain hidden from view. No one writes books about them.'

'Perhaps. But I don't think that was the kind of hiddenness Juan Sebastián intended. Never mind. Let me get back to the matter I raised the other day, the matter of the message. David spoke of a certain message that he bore with him but could not deliver. During his time in the hospital, as I told you, he spoke quite obsessively of it, to me and to other people too. If what you say is true, if he was able to say all that he wanted through the medium of dance, why could he not have delivered this message of his in the medium of dance?'

'Don't ask me, Simón. I am not the right person for such high-flown questions. Maybe it is not in the power of dance to deliver messages. Maybe dance and messages belong to different realms. I don't know. But it always struck me as odd that the disease that killed him began by crippling him. Odd or sinister. As if the disease had a mind of its own. As if it wanted to stop him from dancing. What do you think?'

He ignores the question. 'As you are aware, Dmitri now claims to be in sole possession of the message. Despite the obstructions of the men in white coats, he says, David succeeded in passing on his message to him – to him and him alone. Have you no inkling of what the message may be? Do the children at the Academy have nothing to say about it?'

'Not that I have heard. What they do say, what they seem to accept without question, is that Dmitri was David's most faithful follower. That he was by David's side throughout his last days. That he would have saved David if he could – would have stolen him out of the hospital to some place of safety – but the men in white turned out to be too many and too powerful.'

'Dmitri's associate at the hospital, señora Devito – what do the children say about her?'

'Nothing. All their stories are about David and Dmitri. Dmitri has of course long been part of the folklore of the Academy. No one will go down into the basement at night for fear of being grabbed and eaten by *Dmitri el Coco*, Dmitri the bogeyman with the green hair.'

'Ah, is that who it was, the figure at the concert: *Dmitri el Coco*! How I wish I had never set eyes on the man!'

'If it had not been Dmitri it would have been someone like him,' says Alyosha. 'Such people abound, believe me.'

CHAPTER 24

A LETTER arrives from the selfsame Dmitri.

    Simón,

    I would have preferred to speak to you face to face, man to man, but it is not easy for me to come and go like a normal person, not until consensus is reached that I have paid for my sins, earned my pardon, etcetera. Therefore I write.

    Let us get it out in the open: you have never liked me and I have never liked you. I remember clearly the day we first met. You did not hide your feelings. I was not your type, you wanted nothing to do with me. Yet here we are, years later, our fates as entangled as ever, your fate and mine.

    While David was alive I respected his family set-up. If the story you put out in public was that the three of you were a happy family, father, mother and dearly beloved son, who was I to sow doubts?

    But you know the truth. The truth is, you were never a happy family, never a family at all. The truth is, young David was nobody's son, but an orphan whom for reasons of your own you took under your wing and ringed with a fence of thorns so that he could not escape and fly off.

    Recently I had a chat with Dr Julio Fabricante, who runs the orphanage where David took refuge from you and Inés. Dr Julio is a busy man in his way, and I am equally busy in my way, so it was not easy for the two of us to get together. Nonetheless, we found time to meet and discuss the future of David.

The future of David? you may ask. What future does David have, who is dead?

Here we come to a halt before the question of life and death, death and life. What does it mean, philosophically speaking, at the highest or deepest level, to be dead?

You are a bit of a philosopher in your way, so you will appreciate the force of the question. And I too have become a bit of a philosopher, under pressure of confinement. Confinement, I always say, is the sister of reflection, or half-sister. During my confinement I have thought a lot about the past – about Ana Magdalena in particular, and what I did to her. Yes, what I, Dmitri, *did to her. They keep pushing me, these doctors, to believe that I was not myself when I did it. 'You are not a bad fellow at heart, Dmitri,' they tell me, 'not bad through and through. No, it was this or that that made you do it – a seizure, a fit, maybe even old-fashioned demonic possession of a transient kind. But be of good cheer, we will put you right. We are going to give you pills that will fix you for good. Take one of our pills last thing at night and another first thing in the morning, and behave yourself, and in no time you will be yourself again.'*

Such simpletons, Simón, such simpletons! Take a pill and bow a contrite head and all will go back to being as it was before! What do they understand of the human heart? That little boy knew better. Go away, Dmitri! *he said.* I don't forgive you! *When the doctors were burying me in pills and kindly advice, it was his remembered word that saved me:* I don't forgive you! *How else would I have survived their care and*

181

come out at this end untouched?

The remains of the boy are now bricked up at the orphanage in a wall looking out on a rose garden – a most peaceful setting, Dr Julio assures me. I am not in favour of the fiery furnace myself, but Dr Julio says cremation has always been the policy at his institution, and who am I to question policy? Had I been consulted, I would have voted for burial of the entire physical remains, minus nothing, in an old-fashioned grave. Visiting a hole in a wall, as I told Dr Julio, is never quite the same thing as visiting a proper grave in a proper graveyard, where one can picture the deceased at rest beneath his blanket of earth with a smile on his lips, waiting for the next life to announce itself.

Ashes are so insubstantial compared with a real body, don't you think? And how can you be sure anyway that the ashes that arrive at your address in a modest vase from the crematorium are the ashes of the deceased? But, as I say, who am I to give orders?

I return to the future of David. David was a very special youngster who happened to fall under your care, yours and the señora's, a responsibility to which the pair of you proved yourselves inadequate. Let us not argue, you know it is true. Take comfort, however. We can tell a rosier version of the story of David, one that is kinder to you. It goes as follows. You, faithful, dependable old Simón, were never meant to be more than a minor actor in David's life. Your role was to convey him from Novilla to Estrella and hand him over to me, Dmitri, after which you were to retire from the scene. Have you ever thought of it that way? You are a thoughtful person, so perhaps you have.

You are an honest man, Simón, honest to a fault. Look into your heart. The bitter truth is: I was the one who stayed with the boy through his agony, while you were at home relaxing, having a drink and a snooze.

I was the one who, when the night nurse came with the pills meant to put him to sleep, made the pills disappear. Why? Out of respect for him. Because he feared the pills, feared being put to sleep, feared he would never wake again. Despite insufferable pain (do you know how he suffered, Simón? I don't believe you do), he did not want to die before he had delivered his message.

Not wishing his message to die with him, he chose me to entrust it to. You he would never have chosen. It would have been a waste of time. 'The trouble with Simón is, he does not have ears to hear': that was what he said to me time and again. 'Simón just does not recognize who I am, cannot grasp my message.'

I recognized David and he recognized me. No doubt about that. We were a natural pair, he and I, like a bow and an arrow, like a hand and a glove. He was the master, I the servant. So when the time came for him to die, it was to me, faithful Dmitri, that he turned. 'I am tired, Dmitri,' he said. 'I am done with this world. Help me. Cradle me in your arms. Make it easy for me to go.'

I return to the main point. In one sense, David was carrying a message, though the content of the message is still obscure. Maybe he had not entirely formed the message yet. Maybe there was a cloud in his mind, out of which the message was going to be born. That is possible. But in another sense, whether he had a cloud in his mind or not is irrelevant, since David himself may have been the message.

The messenger was the message: a blinding thought, don't you agree?

That the messenger or the message or both together should end up bricked away in a wall is outrageous. We cannot allow it. I want you to go to the orphanage and remove him. It is not a big job. A hammer and chisel should be enough. Do it after dark. Wait for a stormy night when

183

you will not be heard above the clamour of the elements.

He passed by like a comet. I am not the first to make this observation. A comet is easy to miss: the blink of an eye is enough, a moment's inattention. We owe it to him, Simón, to keep his light alive. I know it does not come easily to you, robbing a grave. But it is not a proper grave, just a cavity in a wall. Look at it that way.

You and I do not see eye to eye on many things, but we have one thing in common: we both love David and want to bring him back.

Dmitri

PS. My mail has to pass the scrutiny of a cabal of doctors, that is how things are run here, so do not address your reply to me. Address it in the care of Laura Devito, a trusted friend and – I might add – a spirited devotee of David. When this sorry business is over and we have a chance to relax over a glass of wine, I will tell you the whole story, the story of her and me. You will not believe it.

He tears Dmitri's letter in two, in four, and drops the pieces in the bin. Curious, Dmitri's power to upset him – upset him and make him seethe with anger. Normally he is a placid man, placid to a fault. Does he seethe because he is jealous of Dmitri, of Dmitri's claims to intimacy with David? *He was the master, I the servant.* Not the words that he, Simón, would use. *He led the way, I followed*: that is what he would say, in respect of himself.

He does not believe Dmitri's claim to be in possession of David's message. If Dmitri indeed has a message, it will be one that he has made up to suit his own purposes – to discredit his judges, for instance, and set him free from the confinement (sister of reflection!) they have imposed on him. Thus: *Blessed be the insolent, for to them it is given to speak the truth. Blessed be the passionate, for the record of their crimes shall be wiped clean.*

Three days after Dmitri's letter there is a knock at the door. It is one of the children from the orphanage: Esteban, the tall, gangly boy with the raging pimples.

Without a word Esteban holds out a letter to him.

'Who is it from?' he asks.

'Señora Devito.'

'Is señora Devito expecting an answer? Because I can tell you now that there is no answer.'

Esteban utters no word; a flush spreads over his face.

'Come in anyway, Esteban. Sit down. Would you like something to eat?'

Esteban shakes his head.

'Well, I am going to make you a sandwich anyway. If you don't want to eat it here you can take it back to Las Manos. I am sure you don't get enough to eat there.'

Cautiously Esteban takes a seat as instructed. He, Simón, slices bread, spreads jam on it thickly, sets it before the boy with a glass of milk. Still blushing, Esteban eats.

'You were a friend of David's, weren't you, Esteban. But you weren't part of the football team. Football is not your sport, I would guess.'

Esteban shakes his head, wiping sticky fingers on his trousers.

'What is your best sport? What is your favourite thing to do?'

Esteban shrugs helplessly.

'Do you like reading? Is there a library at Las Manos? Do you get many chances to read stories, made-up stories?'

'Not really.'

'And what are you going to be when you leave Las Manos, when you grow up?'

'Dr Julio says I can be a gardener.'

'That's nice. Gardeners are good people. Is that what you want to be in life: a gardener?'

The boy nods.

'And Maria Prudencia? You are friends with Maria Prudencia, aren't you? Is Maria going to be a gardener too? Will you be a gardening couple?'

The boy nods.

'Do you remember, Esteban, what you said at the memorial event for David, when you and your friends marched into the Academy carrying the empty coffin? You said that you wanted to pass on David's message. What was the message you had in mind?'

The boy is silent.

'You don't know. Everyone is convinced that David had a message for us but no one knows what the message is. Tell me, Esteban, what was it about David that attracted you? What made you and Maria Prudencia come all the way to the hospital to visit him day after day when he was sick? What gave you the courage to stand up and make that speech from the stage? Because I do not think making speeches comes easily to you. Would you say it was friendship that inspired you and gave you strength? Is that the term you would use? Maria is your friend, anyone can see that, but was David your friend too, would you say?'

The boy contorts his shoulders in a fit of embarrassment and confusion. How he must be ruing the day when he agreed to deliver a letter to the old geezer who pretended to be David's father!

'All right, Esteban, I will stop quizzing you. I can see you do not enjoy it. For years, you know, I was David's closest friend. His welfare was my sole concern, to the exclusion of everything else. It is not easy when a friendship like that is broken off all of a sudden. That is why I ask you about him. So that I can have a chance to see him through your eyes. So that he can come to life again, for me. Don't be cross. Tell señora Devito there is no reply. Here are some chocolate biscuits for you. I will put them in a bag. Share them with Maria Prudencia. Tell her they are from David.'

When Esteban has left he tears up the letter without reading it and tosses it in the bin. Half an hour later he recovers the pieces and lays them out on the kitchen table.

Simón:

I made a simple request, which you have not responded to. You have until Saturday to act, then I will have to ask someone else.

Dmitri

PS I am sure you are aware how unimportant names are. I could just as well have been named Simón, you could just as well have been named Dmitri. And as for David, who cares now what his real name was, that he made such a fuss about?

Things do not work by name, in this hospital or anywhere else in the world. Things work by number. Number rules the universe – that, I can now divulge, was part of David's message (but only part).

You have no idea how casually bodies are disposed of here in the hospital, post mortem. Our profession is life, not death: *that is our proud motto.* Let the dead bury the dead.

David's failing was that he did not have a number, a proper number that he could be tied to reliably. Being without a number is not unusual among orphans. Dr Julio confides to me that now and again he has to invent a number for a child in his care, since without a number you cannot access social benefits. But consider what happens in the dead room (that is what we call it here, the dead room) when a cadaver arrives without a number, or with a number that turns out to be, shall we say, fictional. How do you close a file when there is no file to close? You have a body on your hands, an indubitable physical body with height and weight and all the other attributes of a body, but the person, the being, the entity to whom that body belonged does not exist, has never existed. What do you do, when you are just a lowly corpse-handler, at the very bottom of the hospital ladder? I leave it to your imagination.

The point I make, Simón, is that David need not be dead. Something passed through the dead room that signified the advent of an absence in the world, a new absence, but that absence was not David's, not necessarily, not indubitably. There are ashes, indubitable ashes, in a hole in a wall near the river, but who can say whose ashes they are? Possibly just any old ash swept up off the bed of the furnace, once the furnace had cooled down, and put in a vase. David was wheeled into the dead room: you saw him there, I saw him there. What happened next is all a muddle, a muddle and a mystery. Was he wheeled out? Did he walk out? Did he vanish into thin air? There's no knowing, just as there is no knowing the cause of his death. Atypical *was the word the doctors settled on: an atypical something or other. They might just as well have written,* A malign conjunction of the stars. *Anyway, the file is now closed (there is a big black seal they stamp on a file when it is closed, I have seen it with my own eyes: FILE CLOSED). But whose file is that file, philosophically speaking? Maybe it is just the file of some phantom conjured up in Dr Julio's office for reasons of convenience, in which case it is, philosophically speaking, no one's file.*

Do you see my point? Lots of confusion. Lots of unanswered questions.

As I said, you have until Saturday.

PPS You have never been confined, Simón, so you have no idea what it is like to be cooped up with no promise of freedom. And the company I have to keep! I, Dmitri, among a troop of white-haired old men, crook-backed, slobbering, incontinent! You think the closed wing of the hospital is a better fate than the salt mines? You are wrong. I am paying dearly for my mistakes, Simón. I pay every day. Bear that in mind.

What we want, what all of us want, is the word of illumination that will throw open the doors of our prison and bring us back to life. And when I say prison I don't just mean the closed wing, I mean the world, the whole wide world. For that is what the world is, from a certain perspective: a prison in which you decay into crook-backedness and incontinence and eventually death and then (if you believe certain stories, which I do not) wake up on some foreign shore where you have to play out the rigmarole all over again.

What we hunger for is not bread (that is what we have for lunch every blessed day, bread with baked beans in tomato sauce) but the word, the fiery word that will reveal why we are here.

Do you understand, Simón, or are you beyond hunger as you are beyond passion and beyond suffering? I sometimes think of you as an old shirt that has been dragged through the ocean so many times that all colour, all substance has been washed out of it. But of course you will not understand. You think you are the norm, señor Normal, *and everyone who is not like you is crazy.*

Have you any conception of who the child was who lived under your care? He says you agreed he was exceptional, but have you any idea how exceptional he truly was? I don't think you do. He had a quick brain and was nimble on his feet: that was what exceptional meant to you. Whereas I, Dmitri, formerly a humble museum attendant and now who knows what, in other words no one special, knew from the moment my eyes alighted on him that he did not belong to our world. He was like one of those birds, I forget the name, that descend from the skies once in a blue moon to show themselves to us mere terrestrials before taking off again on their eternal wanderings. Excuse the language. Or like a comet, as I said last time, gone in the blink of an eye.

The streets are full of crazy people with a message for mankind, Simón. You know that as well as I do. David was different. David was the real thing.

I told you that he entrusted me with his message. That is not strictly true. If he had entrusted me with his message I would not be here in the closed wing writing a letter to a man who bores me and has always bored me. I would be free. I would be a free being. No, he did not entrust me with his message, not quite. During his last days he had plenty of opportunities to do so. I would sit by his bedside when my duties allowed and hold his hand and say, Dmitri is here, *and when his lips moved I would incline my ear, ready for the fiery word. But it did not come.* Why am I here, Dmitri? *Those were the words that came instead.* Who am I and why am I here?

What could I say? Certainly not: No idea, young fellow-me-lad. Mis-sent, if I had to say, if it were up to me to hazard a guess. Dispatched to the wrong place at the wrong time. *No, I was not going to spoil his day like that.* You were sent to save me, *I said* – me, your old friend Dmitri, who loves you and reveres you and would die for you at a pinch. You were sent to save Dmitri and bring back your beloved Ana Magdalena.

But that was not what he wanted to hear. That was not enough for him. He wanted to hear something else, something grander. What exactly, you ask? Who knows. Who knows.

The fact is, authentic sinners like old Dmitri were too easy for him. It was types like you that he wanted to save, types who presented him with more of a challenge. Here is old Simón, with his more or less unblemished record, a good fellow though not excessively good, with no great hankering after another life – let's see what we can do with him.

He was too weak, at the end – that was the conclusion I came to after much inner wrestling. Too weak to bring out the fiery word, for you or for me. By the time he realized the end was nigh, the sickness had taken too much out of him, and he no longer had the strength for what was required.

Do you know that at the height of his illness I offered him my blood? Offered a complete transfusion: his blood out, my blood in. They refused, those doctors. It will not work, Dmitri, *they said:* wrong blood type. You don't understand, *I said.* I am ready to die for him. If you are ready to die for someone, your blood will work every time. The passion in your blood burns up the little blood corpuscles, incinerates them in a flash. *They just laughed.* You don't understand blood, Dmitri, *they said.* Go back to cleaning toilets. That is all you are good for.

I blame them. I blame his doctors. I would never have entrusted a child of mine to Carlos Ribeiro. Good enough with broken bones and appendicitis and stuff like that, but in an atypical *case like David's completely uninspired. That is what you need, as a doctor, in these atypical cases: inspiration. No use falling back on the textbook. No textbook will help you when you face a mystery illness. I am not a doctor's backside, but I could have done better than Dr Ribeiro.*

Until next time.

D.

CHAPTER 25

'THERE IS something I have been meaning to tell you, Simón,' says Inés. 'Paula and I have decided the time has come to sell the shop. We have already had an offer. Once the sale goes through we will be moving to Novilla. I thought I would give you advance warning.'

'You and Paula? What about Paula's husband and children? Will they be moving to Novilla too?'

'No. Her son is in his last year of school and doesn't want to leave. He will stay behind with his father.'

'And in Novilla do you and Paula plan to live together?'

'Yes. That is the idea.'

He had guessed long ago that Inés and Paula were more than just business partners. 'I wish you every happiness, Inés,' he says. 'Every happiness and every success.' He could say more, but he leaves it at that.

So this is how the story ends, he reflects afterwards, the story of their little project in being a family: with the death of the child followed by the departure of the woman, leaving the man alone in a strange city, mourning his losses.

He has not been intimate with a woman since the early days in Novilla, when he was working as a docker. For Inés he has never felt physical desire. There are no easy words for what their relation has been: certainly not man and wife, nor brother and sister. *Compañeros* may come closest: as if, from their common purpose and common labour, there had grown up between the two of them a bond not of love but of duty and habit. Yet even as a companion, even in the narrow range of companionship she allowed him, he has never proved good enough for her, never been what she deserved.

When he arrived on the shores of this land, the official who processed him imposed on him the name Simón and the age forty-two. At first it had amused him: the age seemed as arbitrary as the name. But by degrees, with the passing of time, the number forty-two has taken on a fatality of its own. It was under the hopeful star of forty-two that his new life was inaugurated. What he cannot yet see, what is hidden from him, is when the astral sway of forty-two will come to an end and the sway of another number, perhaps darker, perhaps brighter, will commence. Or has that already happened? Did the day his son died mark the closing of forty-two? If so, what is the new age he has graduated to?

He is familiar enough with the mathematics of the Academy to know that forty-two need not be succeeded by forty-three, forty-four, forty-five. As the stars of the Academy's skies dance to their own tune, so do the numbers. The question is: What sort of man will he be – the *he* who goes or used to go by the name Simón – under his new star? Will he cease to be tame, prudent, dull? Will he become (too late!) the man he should have been to be the right father for David: volatile, reckless, passionate? And if so, what will be his new name?

There was a time when he had a soft spot for Alma, third of the three sisters on the farm. How would he be received, old bachelor Simón, if he were tomorrow to pitch up at the farmhouse door, dressed in his best suit and carrying a bunch of flowers, making a stab at courtship? Would he be invited in, or on the contrary would the sisters set the dog on him?

His ruminations are interrupted by a knock at the door. At first he does not recognize his visitor: he takes her for one of the neighbours from the apartment block.

'Yes? What can I do for you?' he says.

'It is me, Rita,' she replies. 'Remember? I looked after your son in the hospital.'

His heart gives a leap. Is fate proposing an answer to the question *Where to now?* in the form of this not unattractive young woman? 'Of course!' he says. 'How are you, Rita?'

'Can I come in?' says Rita. 'I have brought you David's book, the one he lost. We did a big clean-up and I found it in the staff common room, I have no idea how it got there. How are you, Simón? Are you bearing up? I cannot tell you how we miss David, all of us. It really broke our hearts when ... you know ...'

He offers Rita a glass of wine, which she accepts. The book she has brought is of course *The Adventures of Don Quixote*, which since he last saw it has acquired a dark stain on the cover.

'I must tell you,' says Sister Rita, 'I was in two minds. At first I wanted to keep it as a memento; but then I thought, it must carry so many memories for Simón, maybe he should have it. So here it is.'

'I cannot tell you how grateful I am, Rita. Would you believe it, it was out of this book that David taught himself to read. He knew it by heart, the whole of it.'

'That's good,' says Rita.

He presses on. 'Rita, you were with David during his last days. Did he ever speak to you of a message? Did he leave any message behind?'

'Curious that you should ask. Just recently we were discussing David and what he meant to us. Because when you battle to save a patient, and lose, as we did, it is good to learn from it and take a message into the next battle. Otherwise you can get pretty despondent, believe me. In David's case we decided the key to his message was bravery. David was a brave, brave boy who suffered badly but never complained. Be brave, be cheerful in adversity: that was his message, I would say.'

'Be brave. Be cheerful. I will remember that when my time comes.'

'And your wife, Simón? How is she bearing up? She and David were very close, I could see that.'

'Inés is not actually my wife,' he says. 'In fact she and I will be parting before too long and going our separate ways. But certainly she is David's mother, his true mother, even if she does not have papers to prove it. His mother by election. Inés is his mother, and as for me, I acted the part of his father, in the absence of anyone better. Yes, Inés and I will be going our separate ways. In fact, I must tell you, at the moment you knocked at the door I was wondering what the future holds for me. Inés will be returning to Novilla – that is where she is from, she has family there. I will be staying on in Estrella. I have a job of a kind, it is not a great job, but I get satisfaction from it. I am a bicycle messenger. I distribute advertisements to householders. I suppose I will go on doing that. At the moment you knocked I was wondering who would replace Inés in my life. She and I have been together for nearly five years, I have grown used to being with her, even if we have never been husband and wife in the conventional sense.'

Even as he speaks he realizes that he is saying too much, far too much, and evidently Rita feels the same way, for she wriggles uncomfortably in her chair. 'I must go,' she says, rising. 'I am glad I brought the book back. I hope you and Inés find peace soon.'

He ushers her out; from the doorway he watches her neat little figure recede down the corridor.

He flips through the book she left behind. The stain on the cover – coffee? – has seeped through and stuck the first few pages together. The binding is coming loose. But David's fingerprints are all over it, if invisible. It is a relic of a kind.

Gummed inside the back cover is a slip of paper he has not noticed before. It is headed *City of Novilla – City Libraries*, followed by the words:

Dear Children,

We in the library like to hear whether you have enjoyed reading our books and what you have carried away from them.

What is the message of this book? What will you most of all remember of it?

Write your answers below. We look forward to reading them.

Your friend the librarian.

In the space provided, two readers from the time before he, Simón, borrowed the book from the friendly librarian (and then failed to return it) have left their comments.

I liked Sancho, reads the first. *The message of the book is, we should listen to Sancho because he is not the crazy one.*

The message of the book is Don Quixote died so he could not marry Dulcania, reads the second.

Neither comment is in David's hand. A pity. Now it will never be known what, in David's eyes, the message of the book was, or what most of all he remembered from it.